PENTHUSIASM

A Collection of Work by

Seven Monmouthshire Writers

*To Claire
hoping it brings a smile
x
Margaret Nov '17*

Published by Saron Publishers in 2017

Copyright © of each story by the authors 2017
All rights reserved
No part of this publication may be reproduced, stored in a retrieval system, or transmitted, in any form or by any means, without the prior permission in writing of the publisher, nor be otherwise circulated in any form of binding or cover other than that in which it is published and without a similar condition including this condition being imposed on the subsequent purchaser

ISBN-13: 978-0995649538

Saron Publishers
Pwllmeyrick House
Mamhilad
Mon
NP4 8RG

www.saronpublishers.co.uk

info@saronpublishers.co.uk

Follow us on Facebook and Twitter

ABOUT THE AUTHORS

Seven writers have contributed to this volume. They are all members of a small, informal writing group which meets regularly in the King's Head Hotel, Usk, Monmouthshire.

Maggie Harkness was raised in Lancashire, lived in London and now in glorious Monmouthshire. She has worked as a lawyer and a counsellor and her writing reflects her interest in people.

Anna Hitch, Welsh by adoption, moved to Wales more than 40 years ago for a family life of semi self-sufficiency while continuing a career in the NHS.

Steve Hoselitz worked as a journalist before developing a second career as a craft potter, amateur gardener and professional grandfather...

Louise Longworth: 'I have lived all over the place, due to a life spent as an actress, working in the theatre, television and radio. Having settled with my husband and family in Wales, and having taken up writing, I have been fascinated to find so many similarities between the two creative forms, for example in the development of characters and dialogue.'

Gerald Mason is a retired steelworker and twilight antique dealer addicted to fishing.

Margaret Payne moved from London to Wales 15 years ago. Now retired from teaching, she enjoys tai chi, knitting, morris dancing and, of course, creative writing.

Hugh Rose, ex-professional soldier, ex-professional gardener, ex-nomad, fell in love with Monmouthshire 42 years ago.

Contributions

What D'Ya Think? *(Louise Longworth)*	9
The Librarian *(Anna Hitch)*	10
Lucy's Dog *(Gerald Mason)*	11
Old Age *(Steve Hoselitz)*	14
Looking After Malcolm *(Maggie Harkness)*	15
To Begin at the Beginning *(Hugh Rose)*	17
Regret *(Margaret Payne)*	21
Your Car, My Car *(Steve Hoselitz)*	22
Desmond's Overcoat *(Louise Longworth)*	23
Losing Lottie *(Maggie Harkness)*	31
Only A Butcher's Daughter *(Anna Hitch)*	33
Shades of Grey *(Gerald Mason)*	36
Confused *(Margaret Payne)*	37
The First Argument *(Steve Hoselitz)*	38
Hearts of Oak *(Hugh Rose)*	40
A Shrewd Lady *(Louise Longworth)*	44
Just Time *(Margaret Payne)*	46
Clear The Way *(Anna Hitch)*	47
What Brenda Wants *(Maggie Harkness)*	49
Vanishing *(Hugh Rose)*	52
Poetry Reading *(Gerald Mason)*	53
Trip of a Lifetime *(Louise Longworth)*	54
When It Rains..... *(Margaret Payne)*	59
The Talking Sheep *(Steve Hoselitz)*	61
Why Would You Move? *(Maggie Harkness)*	63
The Creator *(Gerald Mason)*	64
Arnold's Ark *(Anna Hitch)*	65
Morning Communion *(Hugh Rose)*	72
Which Way the Rainbow? *(Louise Longworth)*	73
Childhood Memories *(Steve Hoselitz)*	75

Bucket List *(Anna Hitch)*	78
The Day I Gave a Dinner Party *(Louise Longworth)*	80
Second Thoughts *(Hugh Rose)*	81
My Coronation Day Memories *(Margaret Payne)*	82
Keeping Score *(Anna Hitch)*	83
Just a Pebble *(Margaret Payne)*	85
Talking to Jim *(Maggie Harkness)*	87
No Title *(Gerald Mason)*	93
Best Wishes for the 21st Century *(Louise Longworth)*	94
Border Force Christmas *(Steve Hoselitz)*	95
The Problem *(Hugh Rose)*	97
Ollie and Mollie *(Louise Longworth)*	98
Before Christmas *(Steve Hoselitz)*	100
Angela's New Year's Resolution *(Gerald Mason)*	111
The Befriender *(Maggie Harkness)*	113
The Poet *(Hugh Rose)*	115
Fight *(Gerald Mason)*	116
The Dog House *(Anna Hitch)*	117
The Beat of the City *(Maggie Harkness)*	120
Emily Davison *(Louise Longworth)*	121
The Colour Green *(Steve Hoselitz)*	122
Snookered *(Hugh Rose)*	124
Getting On *(Maggie Harkness)*	133
The Glitter Ball *(Louise Longworth)*	134
Farewell, Kevin *(Maggie Harkness)*	135
A Big Birthday *(Anna Hitch)*	137
Memories *(Margaret Payne)*	140
One More *(Steve Hoselitz)*	141
'Word' Discovers 'Music' *(Louise Longworth)*	143
Children of Choice *(Margaret Payne)*	145
Gaily to the Ceilidh *(Louise Longworth)*	148
Diana *(Gerald Mason)*	149
Would Like To Meet *(Anna Hitch)*	150

Run For Your Mind *(Hugh Rose)*	153
Wakes Away *(Maggie Harkness)*	155
The Sculptor *(Louise Longworth)*	156
Tall Tales *(Steve Hoselitz)*	157
A Novice's Guide *(Anna Hitch)*	159
That Ghastly Purple Thing *(Hugh Rose)*	161
All In a Night's Work *(Margaret Payne)*	166
Goodbye Dear Jake *(Maggie Harkness)*	167
Word Play *(Louise Longworth)*	168
The Days of Chars *(Steve Hoselitz)*	170
Sweet Revenge *(Margaret Payne)*	176
No - Really! *(Louise Longworth)*	177
Normandy 1984 *(Margaret Payne)*	179
Music To My Ears *(Steve Hoselitz)*	181
A Fishy Tale *(Louise Longworth)*	183
The Storm *(Margaret Payne)*	184
A Recipe for Success *(Anna Hitch)*	185
The Wedding *(Margaret Payne)*	187
Arthur's Martha *(Louise Longworth)*	188
The Smile *(Margaret Payne)*	190
When I Was Younger *(Steve Hoselitz)*	191
The Sponge Bag *(Anna Hitch)*	193
'Why Didn't You Call Me?' *(Margaret Payne)*	194
Ordinary People *(Louise Longworth)*	196

Penthusiasm

WHAT D'YA THINK?

Written for a North Country voice

Would you say I'm a bit of a poet
because I do rhyming and stuff?
I've studied me dactyls and epics,
but is that considered enough?

I've worked on the stress in me couplets.
All me sonnets have got fourteen lines,
but have they got depth, and a flavour,
and colour - and strength – like fine wines?

I'm trying to write like a poet,
it's hard though, this juggling with words.
At school I was out playing hockey,
poems were only for nerds.

Could I say I'm a bit of a poet?
Is wanting to be quite enough?
'Study the great ones' they tell you.
So you do - and then try your own stuff.

Even Shakespeare would have to start somewhere,
and I know we have him to thank
for his lovely iambic pentameter, but,
did he worry his verse was too blank?

Did he ever have problems with metre,
caesura, or lyrical line?
Oh, if only a speck of his genius
would float through the air into mine!

No – I'd better hang on to my L-plates,
scribble on 'til I go for my test,
But - if they gave me my poetic licence -
would I really belong with the rest?

Louise Longworth

Seven Monmouthshire Writers

THE LIBRARIAN

This piece was placed third in 'Express Yourself', a Welsh Libraries Arts Competition

The library stayed open late on Friday evenings to coincide with late night shopping. The only librarian on duty leaned wearily against the desk; her long brown cardigan draped neatly over the hunch of her shoulders. She pushed her thick grey hair behind her ears and peered around the library through thick glasses. Ten minutes to closing time and only one customer left. She watched him browsing the science fiction section, a lonely old man who enjoyed his regular chats with the sympathetic librarian.

She turned off the lights in the reference section and glided silently towards science fiction, re-shelving books as she passed. Her soft-soled shoes made little noise on the old worn carpet. She glanced around the library again and then studied the old man. He had wispy, grey hair and age spots on the backs of his hands. Slightly past his prime, she thought, but acceptable. A final check of the library confirmed that they were alone, so she moved silently towards him until she was standing directly behind him. She gave a small shiver of anticipation and then a long fine-pointed tentacle shot out from between her shoulder blades and buried itself into the old man's spinal column via the space between his first two cervical vertebrae. As she sucked, her skin glowed with a pale green luminescence and she smiled with pleasure. The old man shrivelled rapidly until he was reduced to a small wrinkled husk, not much bigger than a walnut. She used the toe of her sensible shoe to kick the remains under the lowest shelf of the bookcase that housed the science fiction books with authors S-Z.

She turned off the last few lights and locked the library door behind her. There was a spring in her step as she headed home. She loved Fridays, a pensioner always set her up for a good weekend, plenty of nourishment and no questions asked – almost a social service in fact.

Anna Hitch

Penthusiasm

LUCY'S DOG

The electronic alarm slowly penetrated Joe's brain. It was nine-o-clock in the morning and Joe Williams was having his first 'lie-in' for years. He had spent his first night in his new house. He had also purchased the complete furnishings from the owner and all he had to do was take up residence. The door bell rang.

Joe ignored it - *can't be important,* he thought - *no one knows I'm here*. He had no family to bother him. The bell rang again.

Bloody hell, Joe conjured up some choice words in his mind. He stumped downstairs and snatched the front door open.

'WHAT?'

A little dark-haired girl looked up at him.

'My name is Lucy. I live next door with my Mama and Henry's got into your garden.'

'WHAT?'

'Henry's got into your garden.'

'Who's Henry?' snapped Joe.

'My dog.'

'What - you let your dog get into my garden? Why don't you keep him on a lead?'

'He jumped over the fence.'

'What d'you mean?' asked Joe, calming down a little.

'Henry jumps over the fence every day,' explained Lucy, 'but now the side gate is locked and I can't get him out.'

'I know the gate's locked - I locked it.'

'Why did you lock it? It's not been locked before.' Joe couldn't answer that one, he just locked it because it was unlocked. Twenty-five years in the Armed Forces caused him to think like that. 'Security' had been drummed into him from his first day in uniform.

'Well, you'll have to unlock it,' said Lucy standing her ground defiantly. Joe hesitated momentarily, then realising that he was losing out in the encounter, disappeared in to the kitchen and returned with the key.

'Come on then - let's get Henry out.' As Lucy followed Joe to the gate he became aware that she had a pronounced limp.

'Bumped your leg?' he enquired.

'No.'

'What's the matter with it, then,' asked Joe.

'It's got a funny name,' said Lucy.

'Oh well, let's go and find Henry.' Despite his grumpiness, Joe was curious about Lucy's leg but refrained from asking further questions.

'Here he is,' cried Lucy as Henry bounded towards them. A tiny Jack Russell terrier danced around the both of them, then hurled himself upside down at Joe's feet.

'Rub his tummy, he likes you,' said Lucy. Joe's heart melted, he wasn't used to being liked by anyone.

'I'll, um, leave the gate unlocked if you like,' said Joe.'

'Thank you,' said Lucy. 'You haven't told me your name yet.'

'It's Joe, he replied, trying to overcome the lump in his throat. It had never occurred to him that she would be interested in the slightest.

'I'll tell Mama,' said Lucy as she picked Henry up.

'Off you go, then,' said Joe. He felt strangely moved as he watched her wobble her way down the front path and out onto the pavement.

As time went by, Joe reluctantly admitted to himself that he looked forward to Lucy arriving to rescue Henry, but as yet, although she only lived next door, he had not yet introduced himself to her mother. Joe suddenly realised that he had not seen Lucy for nearly a week. He couldn't get her out of his mind. At the same time, he felt silly worrying as he did, after all, she was only a kid.

Joe came to a decision. Red faced with embarrassment, he called at Lucy's house. As he rang the door bell, his heart started to pound - what the hell was he doing here - what would her mother say? The door opened and Lucy's mum stood there.

'Oh, err, um - I'm Joe - I - I live next door.'

'Yes, I know, Lucy's told me all about you.'

'Oh, I came around to see if she was all right, I haven't seen her for nearly a week.'

'I'm Jan,' said Lucy's mum. 'You'd better come in - I'm afraid she's taken a turn for the worse.'

'Worse?' exclaimed Joe, 'What d'you mean - I didn't know there was anything wrong with her.'

'I expect you've noticed her leg,' said Jan. 'She has bone cancer and it's spreading throughout her body. The prognosis is not good

Penthusiasm

unfortunately.' Tears welled up in Jan's eyes as she spoke and Joe took her in his arms and held her. Neither could speak. When Joe finally found his voice, he asked in little more that a whisper if he could see her.

'Of course,' said Jan, recovering a little, 'she's in her room at the top of the stairs. You go up and I'll make a pot of tea.'

As Joe went up the stairs, he wondered if he would have the strength to maintain his composure. He'd been through some horrendous experiences in the Army. Many times on active service he'd seen good men die and he had become hardened and unemotional. He thought nothing could touch him, but here he was - big man - hard man - frightened out of his wits over Lucy who came into his life because Henry jumped over the fence. His hand trembled as he opened the bedroom door.

'Hi, Lucy.'

There she was, lying in bed surrounded by teddy bears and fluffy toys.

'Joe.' Lucy's face brightened up but her voice was weak. He took Lucy's hand in his, he couldn't speak. 'It's all right, Joe, I'm not afraid, I'm just worried about Mama and Henry when I'm not here.'

'Don't you worry about that,' said Joe, 'I'll look after the both of them - I promise you.'

'Thank you, Joe, said Lucy, 'I won't worry any more.' Lucy died in her sleep a week later.

Several weeks after the funeral, the priest called on Joe just to see how things were going. Joe told him of his promise to Lucy and suddenly felt like talking. He went through his early life - foster homes - minor scrapes with the law until he was old enough to join the Army. He admitted that the army offered him 'security' for the first time in his life, albeit at a price. He was moved to ask the priest a question.

'Where was God in all this?'

'I don't know the answer to that one,' said the priest. 'I've asked myself the same question countless times, but one thing I do know - Lucy gave you the most priceless gift on earth - she taught you how to love.'

Gerald Mason

OLD AGE

Tell me why it's still so cold,
It's April now and Easter's gone
Is it that I'm getting old?
I can't afford the heater on.

I had to work some extra years
Before my pension came along.
My payments are all in arrears.
Thank you, Mr Cameron!

One used to live to seventy five
But nowadays that number's grown
Some of us will be alive
When William V is on the throne.

Old age, they say, is not so bad,
And if you've got a lot of money
You can visit Trinidad
And other places nice and sunny

But some of us have little wealth
We've never had that much to spend
So endless days without one's health
Promise just a bitter end.

The divide between the rich and poor
Is wider than it's ever been
Like the gap beneath my kitchen door
Which lets the bitter winter in

Yes, tell me why it's still so cold
It's April now and Easter's gone
And I have got far too old
It's time that I was moving on.

Steve Hoselitz

Penthusiasm

LOOKING AFTER MALCOLM

'What's the secret of a happy marriage?' Amazing how many times I've been asked that since Malcolm and I celebrated our golden last year. I always say the same thing: 'Look after your husband, a happy man makes a happy marriage.' Course the women's libber types don't like it but what do they know – if women hadn't been so busy having careers and enjoying themselves, we wouldn't have half the divorces. No, my Malcolm's always come first in our house and we've hardly had a cross word – you see, in some ways I know him better than he knows himself so I can always make things just right for him.

Don't get me wrong though – it's not all been plain sailing – I mean you've got to work at marriage, give and take. I remember one year I was booking our two weeks' holiday – the usual guest house in Bournemouth - £30 a night including 3 course evening meal with a choice of starters and desserts and ginger snaps in the room – anyway, I mentioned it to Malcolm and he says,

'Oh, I thought we might go to Egypt this year – have a change.'

'Egypt, what do you know about Egypt?'

'Quite a lot actually, I've got a book.'

'But what about your stomach problems – remember that week in Malaga you never left the lavatory – and we had a lovely view from the balcony. Egypt's a lot more foreign than Malaga – you'd be mad to take the risk.'

Anyway, I booked Bournemouth as usual – it was all for the best. He never mentioned Egypt again.

I've always chosen Malcolm's clothes – I mean what do men know about things like that and I like to see him look smart. Anyway, a few years ago, he decides he's going to get his own stuff – I think it must have been one of those middle life crack-ups – he came back with a pair of jeans and a black leather jacket – said it made him feel young. Only trouble was it didn't make him look young – quite the opposite – the jeans showed off his paunch and the leather gave his skin a bit of a waxy look. I gave it two weeks, then while he was out I replaced them with a nice pair of slacks and a blazer – much more his style. He didn't seem to notice they'd gone – he never said anything.

Since Malcolm retired five years ago, I thought we'd get to spend more time together – go on trips to the garden centre, maybe see a show sometimes. But it's not worked out like that because Malcolm's taken up golf. Don't get me wrong - I'm pleased he's got an interest and as he says, it stops him getting under my feet, but he's hardly here anymore.

When he isn't playing golf, he's going out with his golfing friends ('you wouldn't like it, Joan, all we talk about is golf') and then he goes off for weeks at a time to places like Spain and Tenerife – comes back looking brown and cheerful with bottles of cheap port. He doesn't seem to get his old stomach problems anymore and I've noticed he's started wearing jeans again – at his age! But I haven't said anything.

Malcolm says I should take up a hobby – but what do I want with hobbies – looking after Malcolm and this house takes up all my time and he'll soon get sick of golf – I know he will.

Maggie Harkness

Penthusiasm

TO BEGIN AT THE BEGINNING

With the outbreak of war in 1939, we returned from India, where my dad had been serving in the British army, and were billeted in Southampton. The town later suffered from systematic bombing during the Blitz and my earliest memory is of an air raid.

We were put into a shelter under the stairs behind an iron grille. Mum said it was a silly place for a shelter because the gas meter was there and if that blew up it would kill us all. She put a bolster pillow on top of the meter, sat on it and everybody then felt safe. Aunt Gladys, heroically, put the grille in place from the outside and then went into the kitchen where she got underneath the table, pulling a mattress on top of her.

I was at the back of the shelter huddled up with my sister Cherrie. We were in front of mum, who was keeping the gas meter in place, while in front of us were my other sisters, June and Jean. The house across the street received a direct hit. I can still feel that explosion – a physical force which made even the air vibrate. The front door flew past us to crash into the wall at the end of the passage. Our faces were stung by grit and pieces of debris that had been blasted through the grille. I could see, out of the hole where the door had been, across the street to where a huge fire was roaring. Suddenly I heard Aunt Gladys, from under the table in the kitchen, singing at the top of her voice: '*Onward Christian soldiers, marching as to war...*' This was immediately taken up by my mother and the older girls who sang the complete hymn as loudly as they could, gaining comfort from their defiance.

After this, Mum read the riot act to Dad and the authorities – strings were pulled and we were evacuated to a semi-derelict farmhouse in rural Nottinghamshire.

Snakehall was built of flintstone, its thick walls holding oak beams which supported a grey slate roof. It was reputed to date back to the days of the Danish occupation and owed its name to a Baron who had a snake as his armorial emblem.

Devoid of all mains services; heating and cooking came from an open fire and cast iron range. Lighting was provided by paraffin lamps and candles; water had to be manually pumped from an ancient and cantankerous contraption, set in the flagged stone terrace outside. The lavatory was a thunder box privy situated in one of the barns which formed a horseshoe shape in front of the house. An arched entranceway led through one of the barns to an orchard of apples, pears, plums and an easy to climb cherry tree. This last was my favourite as it became a prop for many adventures – the crow's nest of a pirate ship, a previously unclimbed mountain in the Alps, Robinson Crusoe's tree house and many more places of imaginary wonder. It also produced huge crops of succulent fruits on which we would gorge until our gluttony was punished by tummy aches that had us rolling, in agony, on the ground.

This bucolic setting, which for many years had settled into tranquil decay, was now brought to life by the noise and bustle of inquisitive hands and eyes, eager to explore every inch of its mysterious charms. My mother, who had never truly left her own childhood, became leader of the gang. With her vivid imagination and love of fun, while half the world was intent on killing the other half, she made my wartime memories some of the happiest of my life.

Before our arrival, Snakehall had been thought to be haunted; a place to be avoided for fear of its creepy atmosphere; now, it became a magnet, drawing in children from the village and outlying farms, who wanted to share in our make-believe lifestyle. Many of them stopped overnight and we often had as many as five in a bed; some at one end and some at the other. Their parents were convinced that Mum was not the full shilling but the kids were captivated by this exciting enchantress who flitted about in a sari and produced tureens of food which had mouth-watering aromas. Although nowadays curry has become almost a national dish, in the early forties it was a largely unknown and exotic foodstuff. Mum used to claim that the recipes had been given to her by the servants of the Maharaja of Kutchbawani but in

Penthusiasm

reality they, like her stories, were the product of her ever-inventive mind.

Whenever there was a full moon, we would have a party in honour of the moon goddess Lunora. Everyone would gather in the orchard where we ate homemade scones and drank homemade lemonade before covering ourselves with sheets to dance around the cherry tree, laughing and singing in the silver light. Although I have long known that it was only a name made up by my mother, I still feel compelled by a full moon to go outside and shout Lunora's praises to the sky.

Food was in short supply during the war years and we did everything that could be done to eke out our rations. To this end we made forays out into the surrounding countryside in search of elderberries, blackberries, mushrooms, hazel nuts and rose hips from the briars in the woods and hedgerows. Each of these expeditions was turned into an adventure. We were members of a safari, stalking big game through the African Savannahs. Stick bearers were nominated. This position was jealously sought after and had to be decided by games of dib, dib, dib. The sticks, of course, were substitutes for guns which had to be brought into play whenever Mum, the chief hunter, spotted a tiger in the bushes or a python in the overhanging trees. At the bottom of the field nearest to the house, a brook, which was little more than a rain run-off gully, trickled its inch or so of muddy water across the land. Mum saw no brook but the mighty waters of the Zambezi and great care had to be taken when crossing this raging torrent. We had to hold on to one another in case of being swept away, while the stick bearers had to be especially alert for crocodiles that would grab you in their jaws, then spin around and around as they took you down into the depths. There was also danger from hippos which could eat a whole boy in one mouthful. Whenever we crossed the field on the far side of the orchard, the dairy cows, most of which we knew by name, became dangerous herds of water buffalo or rhinos that could stamp a person flat without even thinking about it. The cows, as is their nature, were curious about our skulking in their pasture and would increase the excitement by following us around trying to nuzzle us with pink, wet noses. The stick bearers were ordered not to shoot the cows as they were important to the war effort. I was never sure what that meant as Cherrie used to use it when we were playing on the rope swing in the main barn. 'I have to go first,' she'd say, 'because I'm important to the war effort.'

In about nineteen eighty four, Cherrie took Mum back to Snakehall. The house had been pulled down, though the base was still there as were the barns and the orchard including the cherry tree. While they were walking around, a young farmer, who then owned the land, came over from a neighbouring field to see what they wanted. As he approached, he called out: 'You ladies wouldn't come up here at night time.'

'Really?' said Mum. 'Why's that?'

'Because it's haunted,' he said. 'A mad woman with lots of kids lived here during the war. If you come here at night, especially if there's a full moon, you can hear them running about singing and laughing and carrying on.'

'Well, I can't see how that could be,' said Cherrie. 'That family was ours and we are all still alive.'

He wouldn't believe them as he swore he had, himself, heard the voices many times.

I'm glad that we have become part of the legend of Snakehall and I would like to think that, indeed there are voices to be heard. Not ghosts, but joyous moments caught in some cosmic recorder to be held in another dimension. So that every time I think of those days my memory pushes a play button; thereby releasing a string of wild haired, barefoot children with sunburned faces, skinned knees and berry stained fingers who, with sheets over their heads, dance, sing and shout their love of life at the ever constant moon.

Hugh Rose

REGRET

Young, free, besotted, and in love, wrapped in promises and dreams.
Prepared to show him her love, by every conceivable means
She chose to take his name, and have it etched in deepest blue.
It would be a constant reminder, to remain faithful, happy and true.
But as the years slowly crept by, his needled name became misty and faded
With two young children cursed in poverty, her dreams began to turn jaded.
When middle aged, tired and bored, she cursed her youthful deed
Packed her belongings, covered her arm so his name she couldn't read.
Now old and wiser and content, she gazes at her arm and a smudgy blue name.
How lucky she had been, finding a new lover whose name was the same.

Margaret Payne

Seven Monmouthshire Writers

YOUR CAR, MY CAR

Your classic car is faded red
And once went fast – or so it's said.
It's now on blocks, the tyres need air,
It's rarely driven anywhere.
The leather's cracked, something drips,
It can't be used on shopping trips.
The gearbox whines; suspension creaks,
The cooling system often leaks.
A blessing if the engine starts;
A nightmare if you need spare parts.

* * *

My car is what a car should be:
Cheap to run, emission free.
A family car (I am no fool),
It always gets the kids to school.
The seats wipe clean, there's lots of room,
Performance wise, its 'vra-vra-vroom'.
You never need to lift the hood,
The ride is smooth, road-holding good.
A perfect choice – there's just one snag:
My car is not *your* E-type Jag.

Steve Hoselitz

Penthusiasm

DESMOND'S OVERCOAT

The trunk was old. Its scuffed but obviously expensive leather and haphazard scattering of faded labels suggested an era of privilege and gaiety, to which he felt the rather grand lady, who had offered the trunk and its contents to the theatre wardrobe, must once have belonged.

Desmond had travelled to the imposing manor house on the local 'bus, and had walked up the long winding drive to the front door, but, after accepting the trunk with gratitude and taking afternoon tea with his benefactress, he had, to his delight, been driven back to the theatre in the glorious old Bentley, by her equally old, and almost as glorious, uniformed and booted chauffeur.

Back in the props room he started to unbuckle the trunk's worn leather straps.

Clicking open the still-smooth brass catch, he lifted the lid. Wow! Even in the dim light of the 40 watt bulb, the exotic colours of the garments inside took him by surprise.

First, he pulled out a sumptuous red satin kimono, lavishly embroidered with butterflies, dragons and chrysanthemums, then a fabulous 'Fortuny' style, pleated chiffon gown of rich purple. Next a swirling gold brocade opera coat, and then an emerald and azure shot-silk creation - a ball gown, he guessed - encrusted with thousands of sequins and twinkling beads.

And then he saw the overcoat.

It lay there, carefully folded, its dark navy blue cloth a sombre backdrop for the rich hues of the gowns tumbling over the edge of the trunk. *Must have cost a bomb in its day,* he thought, as he lifted it out. *It's like something you see toffs wearing in old black and white films.* He slipped his arms into the satin-lined sleeves and turned to look at his reflection in the blotchy old mirror. *Not bad,* he thought, striking leading-man poses, and, having wrestled briefly with his conscience, decided that the coat was meant for him. He'd be a heck of a lot warmer this winter than last year. Anything in the pockets, he wondered, but to his disappointment, they were empty.

Suddenly, the stage door flew open, and the whirlwind that was Polly blew in – red hair flying, green eyes luminous with excitement.

'Hey - get you! You're looking very Cary Grant this morning,' she laughed, as she flew past. 'Wherever did you get that from? You can't have bought it – not on what they pay us! Come on, Cary,' she called back, 'get your skates on, we'll be late for rehearsal. Don't disappear afterwards though,' she ordered, 'I've got something simply amazing to tell you!'

Amused, Des followed the flying figure towards the stage. *What now?* he thought. *What mad idea has she got into her head this time?*

After rehearsal, Polly grabbed him. 'Look, I know you've got stacks of things to do, but I'll help you set up and do props and stuff later. Come on, sit down, you've just got to hear this.'

She bounced on to the lumpy old sofa and sat hugging her knees. Des took the line of least resistance and joined her. 'Right,' she said, 'now - you're never going to believe this, 'cos it's knocked me for six. Get this – my landlady is only a medium! She is, honestly, and yesterday she did a - what d'ya ma-call it? – yes, a "reading". And I went to it. It was incredible. There were about seven of us and she got a message for everyone. One woman's mother came through and told her something only she would know, and - oh yes - this was funny, one guy's ex-girlfriend came through. Apparently he's married now, and what she said didn't half make him blush. Flo got names and everything and told people loads of things they said were true.'

'Did she say anything to you?' asked Des.

'Didn't she just,' said Polly. 'My darling Gran came through and told me things that honestly only I would know. About when I was little and stuff like that. But the clincher for me was when she told me that Gran was saying that my mother fell and twisted her ankle badly last week. I said no, that

Penthusiasm

wasn't right, because I'd spoken to her only yesterday, and she said, oh yes it was and to ring my mum and ask her. And get this - when I did, Mum only said that yes, she had fallen and hurt her ankle but hadn't said anything so as not to worry me. Wanted to know how on earth I knew. What about that? Anyway, Flo's holding another session next week, and you've just got to come. No excuses.'

So a week later, an extremely reluctant Desmond found himself sitting with Polly and seven complete strangers, in Flo's sitting room. It wasn't all spooky and old-fashioned as he had expected. Instead, it was modern and bright, with a log fire crackling and sending out sparks behind the fireguard.

Flo herself was a surprise too. Instead of an old woman with gypsy earrings and flowing robes, she was young and pretty, with long dark hair.

The readings began, and people seemed to be receiving messages from the 'other side', which seemed to amaze and delight them. Des tried to remain detached and analytical, but it was hard not to be affected when people were, by turn, moved to tears or happy chuckles. *I'm still sceptical though,* he thought. *I still can't bring myself to believe it.*

Then Flo turned to him.

'You've got a new coat at home,' she said, 'Well, new to you.'

'Yes, I have,' he said, thinking that Polly must have mentioned the find in passing.

'I know you have,' laughed Flo, 'and it's got something in one of the pockets.'

Gotcha, he thought. 'No, I'm afraid not,' he said politely. 'I checked the pockets and they were all empty.'

'I've got a man here,' said Flo, 'he's tall and dark, with a beard – laughing eyes - a bit like some photographs you see of Edward VII, and he's telling me that you've got his overcoat. Don't worry,' she went on, 'he's perfectly happy for you to have it, but he wants you to know that there is a message in a pocket which needs to be delivered.'

'I'm really sorry, but there isn't,' said Des. 'As I said, I've already checked.'

'Well, check again, he's telling me,' said Flo, 'because there's a secret pocket let into the lining.'

Polly's face was a picture.

After the readings, Des couldn't wait to get back to his digs, and of course there was no leaving Polly behind.

When they got to the red brick terrace, they pounded round and round up all the flights of stairs leading to Des's room at the top of the house. As they rushed into the tiny bedsit, the coat, which was hanging behind the door on a bent wire hanger, swung crazily from side to side, before Desmond grabbed it and flung it on the bed. The two friends, still panting, followed it and started to run their fingers over the lush padded lining. Nothing at first, and then: 'Wait a minute,' yelled Polly, 'there actually is something – yes – just there – feel.' She was bouncing up and down in an ecstasy of excitement, as Desmond carefully lifted out what appeared to be a crumpled letter.

'Go on then,' said Polly. 'Hurry up! Open it. What does it say?'

Desmond carefully unfolded the flimsy pages. The letter was written in pencil, in tiny writing, on tissue-thin paper, probably once white, but now a faded ochre, deepening toward the edges. It was headed *Somewhere in France* and dated *Sometime in September*. This was followed by *Sorry, darling Pa, I know what a stickler you are for accuracy but that's the best I'm allowed to do!*

Des slowly started to read out loud:

Dearest Papa,

Isn't it wonderful that the war is now over? Neither myself nor any of us here at the field hospital could quite believe it when Matron assembled us all and told us that the announcement had been made – it had seemed that it would go on for ever. And guess what – I've been told that I'll be coming home soon. Isn't that the best news! Not sure exactly when though, so don't breathe a word to Mama yet – just keep Mum. (Gosh - a joke!) They say we may even be home

Penthusiasm

for Christmas. Can't wait to see you all, and to get Lolly saddled up and to head out over the hills. Coming? It will be wonderful just to do normal things again. Oh for a bath, and to be able to clean one's teeth in actual running water. Bliss! I can allow myself to think of such things again, now that I'm coming home.

Had a letter from Jack's mother a few days ago. Wasn't that sweet of her? She has heard from him at last and wanted to let me know that he is fine. I worked out from what she said that he is somewhere in France like me. I had a feeling he was. She had to go all round the houses to impart that information, of course, to satisfy the censors.

Apparently he spoke of wedding plans – so he hasn't changed his mind! Now, I know that this is Mama's domain, but I thought just the village church, rather than a lot of pomp – seems right, doesn't it, after everything that's happened in the last four years, don't you agree?

I shall miss the boys out here so much though – they are such bricks, you know, always so cheerful in spite of the cruel injuries they have suffered and the terrible things they have seen. No doubt I shall be nursing some of them when I get back to Blighty. (Yes, I've picked up the jargon!). I intend to keep on with it – no more idling about for me – you soon grow out of all that out here.

Now to Mama. I wrote to her a few days ago in reply to her letter, so she should get it soon. I didn't mention repatriation – I want just to turn up on the doorstep and surprise her. It was lovely to have all the news, (and the latest gossip!). I was chuffed to hear that she had beaten the King at croquet. I'm so glad that you had a lovely time. I know how you both worry about me, but let's face it – the Astors give such fun weekends, which should cheer you up. Even when we have to listen politely to the occasional overloquacious fellow guest of the political persuasion. I've sometimes had to bite my tongue but shall not be doing so in future. (I've developed something of a soap-box attitude out here – it changes one, you know.)

Those parties seem such a long time ago – still, 'nil

desperandum' as Nanny is so fond of saying. I'll soon be carpe-ing the old diem again. (I know what you're thinking – 'nil mangle the Latin!') Dear old Miss Milsom would have confined me to the schoolroom for less, copying out reams of the Iliad, *or something equally riveting! Not that I don't appreciate your liberal ideas upon the education of women. You know I adore you for that.*

Dearest Papa, I love and miss you and Mama so much, and just wish that I could express what's in my heart. Oh rats – the kerosene lamp is spluttering again. And speaking of rats, that's something I shall really really be glad to see the back of.

And now I can hear the Battle-axe approaching for lights out, so I'd better close. (She's not so bad really.)

So, God bless you all.

Forever yours,

Your own,

Alice.

PS. Tell the vicar to start tuning the wedding bells!

Back in Desmond's dingy digs, he and Polly sat silently for a moment, until Polly gulped and said in a wobbly voice: 'Des, that was so absolutely sweet,' and after a pause: 'Are you thinking what I'm thinking? If her Dad came back from the other side, he must want you to give it back to her. You've got to do it, haven't you?'

'Of course,' Des agreed. 'I've got a couple of hours free on Sunday. I'll give her a ring from the box on the corner, to see if I can drop it in.'

'Please, please, can I come with you?' pleaded Polly. 'I'd love to see her face when she hears how we found her letter after all these years. I mean, if she was a teenage nurse in 1918 and it's now 1955, she'll be about, what – mid fifties, won't she? Have I got that right? I wonder if she married Jack? Their kids would be grown up by now. Hey, she could be a grandmother. Oh, how fantastic is that?'

The appointment was duly made, and, 'Lady Alice is expecting you,' said a smiling parlour maid, as she opened

Penthusiasm

the door to the excited pair. 'Please come this way to the drawing room.' She ushered them into a sunlit, yellow room, where an elegant silver-haired woman sat in a well-worn gold velvet wing chair.

After Desmond had introduced Polly, they were invited to sit down and take tea.

'Now, I understand that you have something to return to me?' began their hostess. 'How very intriguing.'

So Desmond launched into the story leading up to the discovery of the letter. Then, carefully taking it out of the folder by his side, he handed it to Lady Alice. The two young actors sat quietly, enthralled, watching her face, as she took the fragile sheets and began to read.

The room was silent, except for the rhythmic ticking of the clock on the chimney-piece.

Suddenly, taking a deep breath, Lady Alice looked up and asked: 'This man, the man the medium claimed to see, did she say what he looked like?'

'Yes she did,' Desmond replied. 'She described him as quite tall, with dark hair, a beard, and humorous eyes. He reminded her of pictures of the old king, she said.'

There was a moment of silence, and then: 'Yes, everyone always said how much he resembled the King,' she said, staring into space.

As she turned to them, Desmond and Polly realised that the upright figure was having some difficulty in maintaining her composure, but then, although her eyes were brimming with tears, suddenly a joyous smile spread across her face.

'My dears,' she said, 'I cannot thank you enough for delivering this precious letter to me.'

'Well, we felt sure that you would be interested to see again the letter you wrote all those years ago,' said Polly.

'Oh no, my dear,' was the reply. 'I didn't write it. I have never seen it before. No, it was written by my daughter, who, as you will have gathered, was a nurse in the first World War.'

'Oh, I'm so sorry,' apologised Polly,' but I expect she would like to see it again, wouldn't she?' she ventured.

'Unfortunately, I'm afraid that won't be possible,' was the

reply. Lady Alice turned away, before saying: 'The troopship in which she was returning home hit a mine in the Channel, and sank very quickly. There were a few survivors, but sadly, my darling Alice was not among them.' She paused. 'The morning after we received the news, my dear husband James also died, when his horse shied at a backfiring car.'

Stunned, the two friends desperately tried to find words to express their sympathy at this cruel double tragedy, but Lady Alice stopped them by saying: 'You two young people have done me the greatest service, by bringing me this letter. It's clear that my husband never found an opportunity to give it to me before his accident.' She paused for a moment, and then went on: 'I have always hoped so very much that he and Alice are together, and now, I am sure of it. It is a great comfort to me.'

She then rang a small bell and said, smiling: 'Today, you have brought me the greatest gift I could ever receive, and now I think it would be appropriate if you would both join me in a celebratory glass of champagne. You see, my daughter and I share not only a name, but a birthday too.

'And it's today.'

Louise Longworth

Penthusiasm

LOSING LOTTIE

I'd never wanted a dog – my life was full: with friends, unsuitable men, and my job in publishing. Then a year ago came the phone call from my friend Sarah, the vet.

'Jas, we've had this gorgeous spaniel brought into the surgery – abandoned, all skin and bone – I thought of you. Interested?'

'I'd love to help but I don't think I could manage ......'

'But she's so sweet, why don't you come and see her?'

And the rest, as they say, is history. I called her Lottie and she smuggled herself into my life and heart. We became inseparable – she even came with me on dates: 'Love me, love my dog.' But then, one day she was gone, must have jumped over the fence. How could she leave me? My lovely Lottie, my special girl. I was heart-broken.

I spent the day searching the village, knocking on doors – but no-one had seen her. I went to our favourite places and called her name until I was hoarse – special treats melting in my clammy hands. Once I thought I saw her, recognising the brown and white coat and glossy ears. I called and bent down to hold her. But then I saw she was a stranger and her suspicious owner whistled her away, presuming I was some mad dog snatcher.

The day after, I travelled beyond the village. It was getting dark and a fine drizzle was falling in the mist when I noticed a battered sign: 'Wild Wind Farm' – I'd never noticed it before. A few yards along the track another sign: 'Strangers, keep out'. Sounds friendly, I thought.

The door was opened by an old man from a Dickens novel: toothless and whiskery, he stood silent and glared at me through hooded eyes.

'I've lost my dog – I wondered...'

'Come in,' he snarled, and pulled back the heavy door which groaned painfully on its hinges.

The room was dim in weak candlelight; an old lady sat in a rocking chair before a huge fire in the old-fashioned range, with three skinny cats asleep at her feet.

'This is Lottie.' I handed her photo to the man. 'Have you seen her?'

'Look Martha – the image of our Jess.' The old lady took the photo and held it close to her eyes. She then placed it on the arm of her chair saying softly: 'Yes, just like our Jess – we lost her years ago.'

'But have you seen Lottie?' I was losing patience.

Martha flashed me a twisted smile.

'No but you'll find her. I can see her behind you.'

I looked round but saw nothing. I'd obviously stumbled on a mad house.

'Martha's got special gifts – she sees things,' the old man said proudly.

'Well, thanks a lot, you are very kind but I must be going.' I ran out of the house and drove at speed back along the track and home. My mind was racing: crazy people - it's all hopeless.

The phone was ringing as I opened the door.

'Hi, Jas, it's Sarah. The most amazing thing – Lottie has just walked into the surgery, I'm sure it's her but she's all skin and bone and there's a name scratched on her collar – 'Jess'.'

I went back to find the farm, but it wasn't there - it really wasn't. I spoke to a farmer nearby and told him of my visit to the farm and asked if he knew where it was. He told me that there used to be a farm there but it burned down at least one hundred years ago. The farmer and his wife, Arthur and Martha, both perished, along with their animals. 'So,' he said, 'you couldn't have met them that night unless you were seeing ghosts......Were you?'

Maggie Harkness

Penthusiasm

ONLY A BUTCHER'S DAUGHTER

Angela Williams was the daughter of the successful pork butcher, Mr JPR Williams. 'Not *the* JPR of course,' he would quip; but the allusion was lost on all but the oldest of his customers. He made a good living but in his old-fashioned way, he didn't consider butchery a suitable job for his daughter, so, whilst Angela was allowed to pack sausages and take the money, he considered the butchering of carcasses strictly man's work.

Angela, or Angel as she was known, with her round face and wide smile, was a firm favourite particularly with the elderly customers, who enjoyed their little chats and admired her thick curly hair which was always threatening to escape from the cap and net required by health and safety. So it seemed a logical progression that, when her father sold the business and retired to the seaside with Edith, an elderly widow he'd been slipping extra sausages to for years, Angel would take a job with the elderly.

She had no trouble getting a job in the local nursing home which had a reputation for providing sensitive care for those elderly people who, whilst still physically fit, had developed dementia. The job interview was a perfunctory affair as Angel had been serving chops and steaks to the Matron for years, though she noted that the chef who prepared the patients' food, bought offal and mince directly from the abattoir. Unfortunately, the nursing home only paid slightly above minimum basic wage, so Angel was forced to devise extra money-making schemes to subsidise her take home pay to make enough to pay her mortgage.

Her first idea for the nursing home was hailed as a green initiative. Angel persuaded the young lad who delivered the patients' newspapers to collect the old ones at the same time and give them to Angel, who then sold them for recycling at a small profit. On the days when Angel was in charge of the paper trolley, she would cancel the papers and just recycle the previous days'. The patients were too mentally confused to recognise the deception and it surprised Angel how quickly the money began to add up. Patients' belongings slowly made their way to the local second-hand shop and she secretly swapped ten pound notes for fivers when giving the patients their pocket money. The drug trials worked well too and netted her far more money for much less work. She just dispensed the additional drugs along with the patients' routine medications; an extra white pill went quite unnoticed in the cocktail of tablets most of her charges were fed every day.

Passing her father's old shop on the way home one evening, after a stressful day, she found resentment bubbling up inside her as she saw how the new owners were prospering. The business should have been hers. It wasn't her fault she had been born a girl. She really needed a good scheme to make her enough money to give up her job at the nursing home and to buy back the butcher's shop.

As she opened the front door, she heard the telephone ringing and reached hastily for the handset before the answering machine kicked in. She glanced at the clock and realised it was 6pm on a Friday evening; time for her father's regular weekly call.

'Hello, my Angel. Have you had a good week?' Her father's cheerful voice was saying the same things he said every week.

'Hi, Dad, how's things with you?' Angel stuck to the regular script. 'How are Edith and her lot?'

'All good here, thank you, though Edith's youngest granddaughter, Tracey's got herself into trouble. Seven months gone and she's only just told her mother and only told her then, because she'd gone into labour. She's at the City Infirmary – tiny little baby – still can't decide if she wants to keep it. Thinks she might put it up for adoption. We'll go and visit her when we get back from the bowls trip to Paignton. Our team's got a good chance of winning this year and Edith and me, we've been practising, so we're in with a chance for the Married Pairs Cup this year.'

Angel barely listened as her father continued to share the minutiae of his new life, letting her mind roam free searching for a money-making scheme, a single big one that would

Penthusiasm

finance her plans and get her out of the nursing home. *Were bowls and bingo compulsory once you reached a certain age,* she wondered? They'd tried to get the residents to play bingo, but most of them were unable to grasp even the basic concept and just dobbed any number they fancied – it was hard to believe that most of them had once lived useful, even successful lives. Maybe she could discover a way to prevent dementia. That would certainly make her the money she needed – fat chance, she thought, what she needed was one big chunk of money; so what could she get her hands on that somebody would be willing to pay a large sum of money for?

In the City infirmary, Tracey was on the post-natal ward, leaning against a pile of pillows and flipping the pages of a magazine. She was on edge, unable to concentrate even on the latest dieting dramas of her favourite soap stars; her grandmother and JPR were coming to visit later. No doubt there would be yet another lecture heading her way. Everyone seemed keen to tell her what she should do. She'd have to make the decision soon. She glanced at the tiny baby that lay in a clear-sided cot pushed close to her bed, his breathing a faint, irregular wheeze. Should she keep it or not, what could she do with a baby, the thoughts went round and round in her head. The door opened and a nurse strode in carrying a cup of tea which she dumped on the bedside locker.

'Here's your tea, love. I reckon you're in the best place today, it's pouring down out there.'

So much for 'team nursing', thought Tracey, putting the magazine down, yet another different nurse. No name badge, so she must be one of those agency nurses. She had to admit though, she quite liked the look of this one with her curly hair, round face and wide smile.

'I'm just taking the baby down for an X ray. OK, Tracey?' Tracey nodded, reached for her tea and returned to her magazine ... as Angel smiled and wheeled the new-born baby away.

Anna Hitch

SHADES OF GREY

I admit it - I've got it - I've had my wicked way
I've bought it - I own it - Fifty Shades of Grey
Having read it once and read it once again,
I now understand simultaneous pleasure and pain

This book proved to me I'm not quite benign.
It stirred memories I thought were long dead.
At eighty years of age things *are* in decline
But E L James hits to spot, it has to be said

E L James is courageous to write such a book
The whole thing depends of a sexual hook
Comedians love it - others pour scorn
Because the reality is - it's nothing but porn

Yes, I would have exploited the world's sexual thirst
But E L James has cleverly thought of it first
She's taken porn from top shelves in the newsagents shops
And introduced us to handcuffs and riding crops.

With no literary value - it's still a success
Seventy million copies sold worldwide
I've heard it described as a 'biblical' sin
I wish I'd written the bloody thing.

Gerald Mason

Penthusiasm

CONFUSED

Never do tomorrow what you can do today
but now look at this another way

If I do today what I could have done yesterday,
I may never have done it tomorrow.

Then if I did yesterday what I want to do today,
I'd have nothing to do tomorrow!!
Confused?

Easy way out,
Just do it when you want to!

Margaret Payne

THE FIRST ARGUMENT

'It bloody well hurts,' he said.

'Don't make such a fuss,' she replied.

'That's easy for you to say, you have just sprung up from nowhere – but I've got this big gash in my side where the rib came out.'

'It'll heal quickly enough,' she said somewhat unsympathetically. 'You men are such babies.'

'How would you know if it will heal quickly – you've only just arrived, so this is the first wound you've seen. And what's more, I'm the first man you've ever met, so how can you say men are babies. In fact, now I think about it, you don't know diddly squat about babies, either... yet!'

'Gracious me. This was not what He told me. I was warned that you'd be lonely and that I had to be nice to you... but I wasn't told you'd be such a cantankerous sod.'

'You'd be a bit crabby too if you'd just had your side slashed open for someone – who then accused you of being a fuss-pot.'

'Well, if you're not going to be more friendly and welcoming, I'll just go,' she said.

'Go? Go? Where will you go? Here we are in the Garden of Eden. That's all there is for now. Where do you think you can go?'

'Oh, I can go all right, misery-guts. I was sent here to have your children and start the human race. But if you are not going to be more agreeable, you can stay here on your own.'

'Have my children? How do you think I can father children with this big gash in my side? He said I was supposed to lie down with you, but I can only lie on one side now. And even then it hurts like Hell. Even if it didn't, I wouldn't be in the mood now...'

'That's no skin off my nose, Mr-so-called-Adam. I don't want to lie down with you, either. Here we are, all alone in this lovely garden in the brilliant, warm sunshine with those lovely apple trees, not a serpent in sight, and all you can do is

Penthusiasm

moan about your health. You clearly know sweet FA about romance.'

'Romance, schromance! If you had sauntered into the garden gently and stroked my brow, maybe wiggled your hips a little and sighed sweetly in my ear and asked me how I was feeling, it might have started out much better. Instead you started by calling me names. Your very first words were barbed. He told me that I'd be giving up a rib for something worthwhile, not for a scold who wanted to leave as soon as she's got here.'

'OK. OK. Let's not go on like this. You *are* rather grumpy, but I admit that perhaps I didn't make the most diplomatic of entrances... I tell you what. Let's try to start again. Pretend it never happened. Here, try this juicy apple...'

Steve Hoselitz

HEARTS OF OAK

'I'll cut you down tomorrow.' Ken shook his fist at the ancient oak as he shouted the threat which he had often made during his youth on his father's tenant farm. The tree had long been a bone of contention between them and the estate's owner, Colonel Masters. Growing in the middle of the field, it made it difficult to manoeuvre machines when cultivating, and wasted a large area of rich, fertile ground.

The colonel would not have it touched. 'Lay a hand on it and I'll have you thrown off the land,' he'd snorted, his face red with anger. 'It's my tree and it stays where it is.'

Ken's father remembered the colonel as a young man when he'd been noted for his social affability. However, since his wife had run off with an American army officer during the war, he'd become an irascible despot, best avoided and never crossed.

Now, long after his parents had retired and moved away to live by the sea, the land was Ken's. The colonel had died, his heirs and successors had sold the manor house, and the farm had been offered for sale. It had meant practically mortgaging his soul but somehow the money had been raised and ownership was his.

He liked to walk out in the evenings, stretching his long legs around his property. His fields ran down the side of a valley to a river whose waters splashed in clear innocence, unlike the brown surge it would become when it tasted the waiting kiss of salt from the estuary's mouth. Ken loved the familiarity of it all. There was a pleasure in knowing every mound and dingle of the place where he had spent his life.

'I'll have you,' he shouted again at the oak. 'Your days are numbered.' He turned and strode toward the house. Behind him, the night closed in, wrapping its fingers in an ominous blackness around the old tree.

Ken had been up early the next morning to feed the stock and now he walked back along the lane into the yard. The sun had not yet raised high enough to produce any warmth. There was a fresh, clean feeling in the cold air which stung his

Penthusiasm

cheeks and made his breath show in puffs of white vapour. He stopped to look at the house that was now his. He could see Molly, his wife, and hear her singing through the open kitchen window where she was peeling apples in preparation for one of her legendary pies. Ken felt good. It was a grand morning, the farm was his and he had a beautiful wife. He suddenly did a little-boy dance in the yard out of the pure joy of being alive.

'Hey you, daftie! What are you doing?' Molly threw an apple core through the window at him. 'Get yourself in here and have your breakfast before I give it to the dog.'

While he ate, Ken talked about cutting down the oak. 'I'll have a go at it tomorrow when Daniel's with me. We can hitch a chain and cable from the trunk to the tractor.'

He gestured in the air with a piece of toast. 'The trouble with those hollow beggars is that you can never be sure which way they are going to fall. If there's a cable on it from the tractor, then it should go in that direction.'

'You and that blessed tree.' Molly wiped her hands on her apron. 'Whatever you do, be careful. I don't want you getting injured just because you've got an obsession with the poor thing. It's a grand old gentleman; I think you ought to leave it where it is.'

'Oh, don't you start.' Ken patted his stomach in content. 'I doubt we'll have much trouble with it. When we've got rid of the wood, I'll get Will Morgan to come over with his JCB. We'll rip the stump out and then there will be much more room in that field for crops.'

'Well, just remember to keep Saturday free,' she said, wagging her finger in his face. 'You promised to come into town with me to help choose a new outfit for our Maureen's wedding.'

Ken groaned and they made faces at each other as he went off out to continue with his day's work.

There was a strange feel to the day. The air was still. No birds sang and the little creatures stayed underground in their burrows, reluctant to emerge into the uncanny atmosphere.

Ken and Daniel worked in silence, shackling up chain and cable to the tractor whose steady throbbing produced the only sound in the otherwise hushed valley.

The oak which had stood in mighty grandeur for several hundred years was no longer a pretty sight. The great girth was covered with thick stems of ivy and bryony, and its once-majestic crown was now decimated. A stag's-head array of dead, blackened branches gave evidence of a long-ago lightning strike. Although it still had a few leaf-bearing twigs, and even, heroically, sported a scattering of acorns, the tree was dead, a wooden monolith, well past its time.

The chain saws snarled angrily as the cruel teeth ploughed into the wood. Progress was slow, for the oak had almost fossilised with age into an iron-like consistency.

'Hell's bells!' exclaimed Daniel. 'I've sharpened my chain twice already and we haven't even got it down yet. We'll be at it all day if the top is as hard as the trunk.'

'Ay!' grumbled Ken. 'The old devil's being a blasted nuisance right up to the end.'

Eventually, however, the tree gave a groan, a howl of outrage and then, with a monstrous sigh, slowly fell over in line with the cable attached to the tractor. The ground reverberated from the impact and broken pieces of timber leapt and bounced across the field.

'What the blazes?' Ken looked in horror at what had been uncovered. Inside the hollow bole, amongst a mixture of soil, moss and leaf litter, was a remnant of rotted sacking from which protruded the skeletal remains of four human feet and legs.

The crows, which up till now had been quiet, began to call.

Ken and Molly pushed their way through the thronging crowds. The town was busy and buzzing with activity as the dozens of stalls in the grand old market hall had drawn in people from all over the county.

Molly was happily laden down with carrier bags. They had been into every dress and shoe shop and, it seemed to Ken, had tried on every dress and shoe in town. Although dog-

Penthusiasm

tired from many hours of questioning at the police station, Ken had dutifully oohed and aahed at each of Molly's selections and then bitten his tongue when they had returned to the first store to buy the first outfit she had seen.

They made their way into the market café where they found a table and ordered refreshments.

'Well, who'd have thought it?' said Molly, blowing at the froth on her espresso. 'That old colonel, shooting his wife and her lover, then putting them down inside the hollow oak.'

'Yes.' Ken frowned with a faraway look in his eyes. 'No wonder he didn't want the tree touched. You know, I disliked him for a lot of years but now I feel quite sorry for the poor chap.'

'I know what you mean. It's a shame really, him so miserable all those years.' She pulled her purse out of her handbag. 'Remind me to go into the building society before we go home. I want to open a savings account.'

'Why? How much are you going to put in?' Ken was alarmed, having already spent more than he had anticipated.

'Don't worry,' laughed Molly. 'Only a tenner. You know what they say – from little acorns mighty oak trees grow.'

Hugh Rose

A SHREWED LADY

Katherine, an heiress from Padua, was known by her nickname – 'The Shrew'
'til her 'taming' by husband Baptista, who'd an eye on her cash! Sad, but true.

He humiliated her, really cruelly, with his bullying and mean double-speak.
Confused her, and starved her, so brutally, that she finally gave in – became meek.

One day she woke up in amazement, for she'd travelled through time, to today,
found herself in a 'Beckham Towers' bedroom, and panicked: what would hubby say?

To go out I must ask permission - his curfew is there to be kept.
The poor girl – so scared of the tyrant – put her head in the pillow and wept.

But then, into the bedroom swept 'Posh', saying: 'Up you get, Kate, we're going up West.
'We're hitting the shops – first it's Harrods – then we'll steadily work through the rest.

'We'll stop to take lunch at The Ivy - next it's facials – then hair by Nick Clarke,
'manicures, massage and foot rubs, then, bubbles! - feet up - in Hyde Park.'

'Won't your husband need first to approve it?' asked Katherine, then stepped back in shock
as her hostess squealed loudly with laughter: 'What? Approve every diamond and frock?

Penthusiasm

'I'm "Posh Spice", not "Mrs D Beckham" – I'm nobody's "mistress", so there,
'any fella says different – they're mincemeat. I can sort 'em –
I'm known for my stare!

'We girls have the ultimate weapon, like those Spartan girls used, to win through.
'Stay with it, Kate! – use your noddle. What can't he have without you?

'Oh, come on, catch up! NOW she's got it! If he wants all the fun, and an heir,
'he must stop all this chauvinist nonsense, show respect and start being fair.

'Look, I'll set up a meeting with Justin, he'll sort the spondulicks for you,
'get your rightful cash back in your purse, kid – and get you a bank card or two!'

So - Katherine stayed on for a fortnight, learned all about Women's Lib laws,
Made her decision. Stuck to it, and said:
'Stuff that! I'm staying, up yours!'

Louise Longworth

Seven Monmouthshire Writers

JUST TIME

The future, the past, the present,
they are all a point in time,
Moving in and out of place,
in a never ending line.

Some people revel in their past,
and wonder where things went wrong,
saying why didn't I do this and that,
and where do I belong?

Others look to the future, and hope
their dreams soon unfold,
saying one day I'll do this and that,
yes, one day before I'm old.

Then some like me, just prefer
to enjoy this moment at hand,
saying I'll try out this and that,
without it being planned.

To revel, to look or to enjoy,
regardless, time marches on.
It always has and always will,
even when we're gone!

Margaret Payne

Penthusiasm

CLEAR THE WAY

The snow fell on Tuesday night. When Wendy woke on Wednesday morning, the world was white. The car was just a hump beneath the snow and the only footprints on the drive were from the neighbour's cat. She wasn't surprised; the weather department had been issuing dire warnings for days, so Wendy was well prepared.

As usual, she took Gordon a cup of tea in bed.

'They were right,' she said as she dumped the mug on the bedside cabinet.

'Who were?' Gordon's voice was thick with sleep.

'The weather forecasters were right, for once. It's thick snow out there. Did you remember to pick up the bread and milk on your way home - like I asked?' Gordon's silence was all the confirmation she needed. He hadn't of course, though for once, she held her tongue.

'Never mind, we can manage; I'm sure the company will let you have one 'snow' day without counting it as annual leave. I'll clear the drive this afternoon and with any luck it'll be gone by tomorrow and you can go to the office.'

As usual, Wendy cooked the breakfast, stacked the dishwasher and tidied the kitchen. Gordon ate his breakfast and then, taking his coffee cup, began to work half-heartedly at his laptop.

'I'll email the office and let them know I'm working from home today.' Gordon heaved up his pyjama bottoms and tied his dressing gown cord tight around his sturdy middle; then he dumped the remains of his coffee into Wendy's clean sink and left the dirty cup on the worktop.

Once she'd made Gordon's elevenses and prepared the lunch, Wendy wrapped up warm and went to clear the drive. That nice Derek Brockway had promised her that there would be more snow tomorrow, but Gordon would have to go to work anyway. She shovelled and sang quietly to herself, enjoying the silence. No traffic noise, just twittering birds and the hum of the heating boiler as it puffed plumes of steam out of the chimney.

Seven Monmouthshire Writers

It took her almost two hours to clear the snow from the drive. A final sluice with a bucket of water washed the windscreen clear and left the driveway slick and black in the sunshine.

Wendy delivered Gordon's afternoon tea to the study, where he was engaged in mortal combat on one of his many computer games.

'I've done the driveway, love; please will you go to the shop and get the bread and milk. The shop's open until 7 tonight.'

'I'll just finish this game, then I'll go and get your stuff. I can pop into the pub on the way back. We'll eat late tonight, after I get back.'

Gordon finally left at a run at five minutes to seven. Not much chance of getting the shopping, but the pub would be nice and warm, so he just grabbed his keys and a bright red fleece and roared off in the company car; snow free and with a clear windscreen.

Supper time came and went, so Wendy did what she frequently did. She put his dinner into the oven and made herself a milky drink and some toast which she ate in the sitting room. She watched television until bed-time, then turned down the spare bed and put a blanket and a pillow on the sofa, so he would have a choice when he finally got home. She slept well despite the overnight drop in temperature and the daylight was bright through the curtains by the time she woke. After dressing quickly in the morning chill, she checked both the spare room and the sofa but there was no sign of Gordon. She gazed out of the kitchen window while she made herself a cup of tea. The forecasters had been right. The drive was once more shrouded in snow – but this morning there was an extra, small pile of snow, with a slight pink hue, between the buried car and the dustbin, exactly where the water had flowed yesterday when she had cleared the windscreen. She drank her tea, then poured herself a second cup and considered. What should she do next? Clear the drive or make the telephone calls?

Anna Hitch

Penthusiasm

WHAT BRENDA WANTS

Aged eight

My friend Hilary who lives across the road gets called in for her tea at the same time every day when we're playing out. Her mum shouts 'Hilareee – your tea's on the table' and she's always smiling like Hilary's dad who goes to work on his bike and smokes a pipe – they're always cheery as if they really like one another and are happy. The only time they were sad was when Hilary told me that she'd had a blue baby sister but she died before they took her home. But soon after that, they seemed quite happy again and Hilary got called in for her tea just the same. I'd like to have a family like Hilary's, where your mum and dad aren't shouting at each other and your mum's not crying all the time. It's only since I've known Hilary that I found out not all families are like that and it sort of makes things harder, wanting things to be different. I sometimes wish that I was adopted and one day my real family would come and collect me and they'd be happy, smiling people who loved one another and I'd be called in for my tea at the same time every day and we'd all sit down together and chat about things. There wouldn't be any shouting.

Aged forty-eight

I can't say what I want – I mean once you have kids, it's not about you any more. I just want them to be happy, that's all that matters. They're both at that funny age – Jason's sixteen and Tracey's fourteen – when I can't seem to do much that's right for them. I only really see them when I'm putting food on the table because the rest of the time they're out with their friends or up in their bedrooms playing music. I wish we were closer, but it's only a stage, they'll come back in the end. It doesn't bother Brian, but then he works all hours and travels a lot or he's out at the pub playing darts with his mates, and if I'm honest he and the kids have never been that close – it's the sort of man he is, not very expressive. I sometimes wonder why he got married because family life doesn't really suit him – he never wants to join in anything and it was always me arranging any days out or holidays when the kids were small – he just wasn't interested. I'm sure he loves us really but he can't manage relationships; they're like a foreign country.

Before Jason was born, I had a job working for the council, secretary to one of the bosses – I was good at my job and I got on well with people there. My boss used to call me 'brilliant Brenda' – I always got a bit of a thrill when he said it. But then I gave up work – I mean, you shouldn't have kids unless you're prepared to look after them properly – and devoted myself to my home and family. If I say so myself, I did it well – regular home cooked meals, spotless house, making the money stretch and putting up with Brian. So I don't think much about what *I* want – my reward is seeing my family healthy and happy – that's all that counts.

Aged sixty-eight

I was thinking the other day how strange it is that the people closest to you never call you by your name. It's always Mum (though since Jason moved up in the world he's calling me Mother) or Nana or as Brian used to call me, 'old girl'; never Brenda. But then that's who I am to them; it's the relationship that matters and that's what I've always believed in. Brenda's never really come into it. At least, she didn't until about two years ago when the bombshell landed one Tuesday morning. I got a phone call from a woman who said her name was Sylvia and she'd just discovered that her husband Brian had another wife and family living on the other side of Manchester and she thought she should get in touch. She'd been married to Brian for fifteen years and they had two children. I remember standing there feeling my knees go weak and wondering how the bugger had managed it – this silent, solid man who didn't seem to like families had gone and got himself two at the same time. Anyway they gave him eighteen months in prison and he went to live with Sylvia when he came out – she was more forgiving than I was.

Penthusiasm

So now I'm on my own and I need to think more about Brenda and what she wants but I'm a bit out of practice after all these years. When I was little, I just wanted peace and quiet, living in a house that was like a war zone; but now I've got too much peace except when the grand-kids are here. I feel the need to make a bit of noise, to stir things up and find something which is all about me and what I'm good at - I'd love to be brilliant Brenda again. So I've started enrolling for things – ballroom dancing is one of my favourites – I'd forgotten how much I loved dancing 'cos Brian was never interested. I've even found a dancing partner – called Donald – I think he's got ideas about us but he can keep them – he's eighty-three and wanting a cook and nurse for his old age. Not a chance – I've done all that and now it's time for Brenda to see what she's made of.

Maggie Harkness

VANISHING

Things that I thought would last forever
were transient
and like those thoughts melted into ether.
Some - deep rooted and evergreen
dissolved and might never have been
like the many people I treasured
and held so dear.
All flit as if fugitive phantoms
then disappear
out of this temporal life I've made
from which all I've loved must fade.
The fleeting triumphs and
what seemed eternal joys
blazed sunlight before
flickering into the voids
of time's catacombs where
nothing is immortal there.
Nothing that is unless
you count the awful nothingness

Hugh Rose

Penthusiasm

POETRY READING

He rose from his seat and adjusted his hat
With a flourish he walked to the stage
He arrogantly fluffed his bright pink cravat
And a voice from the back said: 'Sit down, you prat.'

Cradled in his arms a leather bound tome
Which caused the audience to inwardly moan
As he started to read he adjusted his hat
And a voice from the back said: 'Sit down, you prat.'

He ignored the remark and continued to read
Page after page of monotonous screed
As he read he adjusted his broad brimmed hat
And voice from the back said: 'Sit down, you prat.'

The man on the stage turned bright red with rage
But he continued to read - page after page
He fluffed his cravat and adjusted his hat
And a voice from the back said: 'Sit down, you prat.'

The man with the hat closed his leather bound tome.
He stepped down from the stage and walked to the back
He punched the voice on the nose - then adjusted his hat
And said to the voice: - 'Take that, you prat.'

Gerald Mason

TRIP OF A LIFETIME

Molly and Joe stood outside the theatre, holding hands, as the rest of the audience spilled out onto the pavement behind them, and the traffic of the West End swirled around them. Taxis wove deftly through the melee, motor bikes swerved recklessly in and out and a police car, lights strobing and siren blaring, cut its way swiftly through it all somewhere nearby, followed by an ambulance.

'Bit noisier than the village,' yelled Molly, over the racket.

'You can say that again,' Joe shouted back.

'OK – Bit noisier than...' she began again, giggling.

'All right, clever clogs – heard you the first time,' he called back.

'What now?'

'Taxi, I think,' Joe said, starting to raise his arm.

They were in luck. Almost immediately a taxi drew up. 'Look Joe, it's white,' said Molly, 'like a wedding car. Appropriate or what for today?'

'Where to, guv?' said the driver.

'Well, we were going straight back to St Pancras, but now......' Joe began.

'We'd like to make it last a bit longer,' said his wife, 'make the most of it while we've got the chance. Who knows when we'll be here again. How about a guided tour, love?'

'Why not?' said Joe, 'let's go mad – can't take it with you, can you? So if that's all right with you, driver?'

'Fine by me,' he replied. 'Guided tour it is then.'

'But what shall we call you?' said Molly. 'We can't keep calling you 'driver', can we? Doesn't feel right.'

'Mike,' he replied, 'call me Mike. Here we go then. The Guided tour, according to St Mike ! Hold on to your hats,' he said and swung the vehicle effortlessly round to face in the opposite direction.

'You can turn these monsters on a sixpence, can't you?' said Joe in admiration. 'Modern miracles, aren't they?'

'Certainly are,' Mike replied. 'You've hit the nail square on

Penthusiasm

the head there. Right then, here we go, both. Had a good day then, have you?'

'Brilliant, haven't we?' said Molly. 'We've been to Harrods, of course – you loved that, Joe, didn't you?' Joe groaned in mock pain. 'Then we went to feed the pigeons in Trafalgar Square, went to the National Gallery – wonderful exhibition on there. Joe wanted to go to the Science Museum so we did that – right up your street that was, wasn't it, and managed to fit in a meal at a lovely Italian restaurant before we flopped in Hyde Park. Oh yes, and we saw the Changing of the Guard at the Palace. So much. Then of course to the theatre, which was just wonderful.'

'And that's where I came in,' grinned Mike.

'Right out of the blue to our rescue,' laughed Molly.

'Did you enjoy it, love?' asked Joe.

'Didn't I just. I thought it was amazing, didn't you?' said Molly. 'I know there were some really sad bits but it was hilarious in parts. All those different characters, fascinating. A saga, I suppose you'd call it. And of course the twist at the end. I really wasn't expecting that, were you?'

'Don't know about that,' he laughed. 'I've never known what to expect since the day I married you!'

'Nor sure how to take that,' she giggled, 'cheeky beggar. I'll let you off, but only because today's our anniversary. Normal warfare will resume tomorrow! But, seriously, love of my life, it's been lovely, and it's all down to you.'

He blushed in the darkness. 'Get on with you,' he said.

Mike was a good guide, making sure they saw everything. Westminster Abbey, the London Eye, the Houses of Parliament, Cleopatra's Needle and the Tower of London; the works in fact.

Molly sat close up to the window. 'Oh look, Joe. Isn't it marvellous, sitting here, looking out? The lights, the theatres, the bridges all lit up and the reflections in the river – it's magical, and – oh look – there's the Ritz. Hey, that's what we're doing, isn't it – puttin' on the Ritz! And all those people. I wonder where they're all going? Funny to think of all those different lives. We're looking at them now as we pass, but we're never going to see their faces again, are we? Weird, isn't it?'

Joe sat quietly, a big grin on his face, enjoying Molly's reactions as much as the sights.

'But the icing on the cake was turning into Piccadilly Circus and seeing Eros! I mean, Eros! How appropriate is that for a 50th wedding anniversary!'

Joe smiled. The moment had come. 'Mol,' he said, taking her hand and putting it to his lips. He'd practised this bit. 'Mol,' he repeated, 'I know I don't say a lot, I know that, but I do love you, you know.' He took a deep breath. 'All my heart and all that.'

Molly's eyes were moist. 'And I love you too,' she said. 'In fact, I'll love you forever - and ever and ever and ever. Even if you drive me potty sometimes, you silly old goat'

They smiled at each other, and Mike took a quick pleased peek in the mirror.

'Well,' he said, 'I think that's about it. I think you seen just about everything on offer. Better get off and find good old St P for the next leg of your journey.'

'Thank you so much, Mike,' said Molly. 'My only complaint is that I can't do it all again.'

'Glad to have been of service,' said Mike, 'nearly there now, just around the corner. And – here we are, at your destination. And plenty of parking.'

'How much do we owe you?' said Joe, getting out his wallet.

'You don't owe me anything,' said Mike. 'It's on the house, as they say. My pleasure.'

'But you must let us, Mike,' said Molly, 'you've given us the perfect ending to a breathtaking experience.'

'Just seeing how much you got out of it is payment enough for me,' he replied, 'I don't always see that in my job. It's been a pleasure to drive you two.'

'I'm overwhelmed,' said Joe, 'that's really kind of you.'

'What an angel,' said Molly, leaning over and giving him a kiss on the cheek. 'You're a saint, you really are!'

'That's me,' he chuckled. 'Anyway, you'd better get on

Penthusiasm

your way, hadn't you?' He got out and opened the door for them.

Molly and Joe got out and stood there for a moment.

'Goodness, I thought the West End was bright but this is brighter than any sunset I've ever seen,' said Molly, 'and it's gone eleven.'

'Everybody says that,' said Mike.

'Beautiful though, isn't it, Joe?'

'Certainly is.'

'Now then,' began Mike, 'just to put you in the picture. Contrary to public opinion, there are no pearly gates, sorry. But I do see my colleague St P as I like to call him, approaching fast with your welcoming committee. Goodness me, you're a popular couple, there are dozens of them. There'll be lots of familiar faces there then! Oops! Hang on, there goes my bleeper. Head office calling.'

'Evening, Michael,' said St Peter, striding towards them, 'got another call?'

'Yup, another incoming,' replied St Michael, 'I'd better be off. 'Bye you two, I'm leaving you in the more than capable hands of St Peter. Don't worry, he's an old hand at this, aren't you, Peter? He'll look after you.'

'Certainly shall,' smiled the saint. 'We'll soon get you settled in – and there are a lot of people waiting eagerly to see you. Couple of dogs and a ginger cat insisted on coming too.'

'I feel like I felt on my first day at school,' whispered Molly.

'Me too,' Joe whispered back.

Back where they had come from, a crowd had gathered, as the cacophony of sound carried on around them.

At the roadside, two paramedics looked at each other and shook their heads, then gently placed the two bodies on to stretchers and carried them to the ambulance.

The police had started to question bystanders in the hope of finding witnesses to what had happened.

'Excuse me, madam,' a constable said quietly to a shocked-looking woman. 'I can see that you are upset, but may I ask if you saw what happened?'

'I did,' she replied, 'They just stepped out. I noticed them because they were holding hands and I thought they looked so happy. They were just looking at each other. And then they stepped out... They didn't see the van coming. He tried to brake but they just stepped out right in front of him. It's so sad.'

'Thank you, madam. That's very helpful. If you wait here, I'll organise a cup of tea from the theatre café and then I'll ask you to sign your statement.'

As she waited, crowds thronging past, little heed was given to the white taxi sailing serenely past, on the other side.

Louise Longworth

Penthusiasm

WHEN IT RAINS…..

When it rains in the refugee camp at Polhena
the entrance becomes a pool of yellow slimey mud
Here in Chepstow the pavements and paths are wet but
the drains take away any surplus water.

There, the children still play in the warm rain, heads and feet bare.
Here, we wrap them, boot them and encourage them to play indoors.

There , the adults gaze at their surroundings. Their private thoughts beyond our imagination. No plans.
Here, we gaze at the wet day and generally complain about it. We can't hang the washing, weed the garden or visit the park.

There, the mangy dogs curl up in the rubbish to stay dry
Here, they are indoors, fed and cosy in their beds.

In Pohlena rain drops bounce from the steamy corrugated roofs, sometimes not relenting for days
Rain drops splash on our windows and we wonder if it will stop soon so that we can go out.

Inside their tiny shacks, there are scruffy white plastic chairs
Here, these white chairs are stacked in our sheds for the summer ahead.

They have a bare dim light bulb suspended from a precarious nail above. Only one.
Here, we adorn our bulbs with a profusion of shades in every room and landing. As many as we like.

On colder wet nights they wrap up, cuddle the children and sleep early
We switch on the heater, and the tv. Make hot drinks and read to the children.

Seven Monmouthshire Writers

When it rains in Polhena they smile at visitors, invite you into their shacks. Send the children to buy you a bottle of pop. Offer a chair.

In Chepstow we hope visitors don't turn up today, with their muddy boots and dripping coats because we'll have to clean the hall again.

Margaret Payne

Penthusiasm

THE TALKING SHEEP

Breaking news... 05/02/2017
Almost exactly twenty years ago, Dolly the sheep came into the world, a lamb with a difference, the first mammal to have been cloned from an adult cell.

Now scientists at the same British research institute have perfected another technology, implanting a human brain into a sheep and creating the world's first sentient, talking non-human.

Barbar can reason, talk though an implanted voicebox and even understand random questions from the team who created him here in Midlothian at the Roslin Institute, part of the University of Edinburgh.

Today's breakthrough is certain to cause even more controversy than that surrounding his illustrious ancestor. For although Barbar is, on the outside, still very much a sheep, complete with woolly coat and cloven hooves, by using a mixture of cutting edge transplant and genetic modification techniques, on the inside he is disarmingly human, able to discuss issues with the lab team who created him.

Two decades ago the birth of Dolly seemed to be one of those moments in scientific research that would change the world forever. The cloning of the first animal from an adult cell was a remarkable scientific achievement. It promised new treatments for debilitating diseases. But it also raised fears of cloned human beings, designer babies and a dystopian future.

Now, twenty years on, neither those hopes nor the fears have been realised. But Barbar seems certain to change all that, prompting a whole series of new fears and hopes, just at a time when robots and cybernetics and artificial intelligence are making headlines.

The news of this extraordinary and controversial development has come from a secret recording of Barbar which was apparently smuggled out of the Scottish research lab a few days ago.

In the video, which the editors at ITN have seen but which

cannot be broadcast for copyright reasons, Barbar can be seen answering simple questions, often using slightly archaic language, a trait which is presently puzzling his team.

In the recording made immediately after he was professionally clipped, he is asked if he 'has any wool', to which he whimsically answers: 'Yes sir, yes sir. Three bags full.'

So this extraordinary black ram even appears to have assessed the amount of wool being taken from him and he goes on to indicate who he would like to have the fleece. Posssibly anticipating the immense value that wool from his back will have to both the scientific community for analysis and to curio collectors, he says that he wants the wool shared between the researchers themselves (whom he describes as his master); 'the dame', probably an oblique reference to Her Majesty the Queen; and 'the little boy who lives down the lane' – part of the answer which has, at present, totally baffled scientists.

*This is Steve Hoselitz, for News at Ten,
outside the Roslin Institute, Midlothian.*

Penthusiasm

WHY WOULD YOU MOVE?

Why would you move, you've a lovely view
Why would you move, you've a downstairs loo
You've all that you need and you're getting old
Moving house is for the young and the bold
You're safe where you are, don't take a chance
At this stage in life there's no place for romance
But then you'll be nearer the shops you say
That could be wise 'cos there'll soon be a day
When you can't get about and you're banned from the road
So having things handy could lighten your load
What's that you say? It's a change that you crave?
You want something different and a need to be brave?
It's time to break free and try a new place?
Well I only hope you don't fall flat on your face
Getting old is for settling and staying put in the known
You should count yourself lucky and rest in your home

Maggie Harkness

THE CREATOR

Where now is this Supreme God that loves us — allegedly
The creator of the universe and everything within
Here am I — born into catholic pomp and ceremony
lndoctrinated, enculturated and immediately guilty of mortal sin
Am l being punished for leading a happy life
Am l to retain my faith when illness falls upon my wife
ls this some devious testing of my allegiance
By a god I never see or hear who ignores my cries for help
And what of priests who walk among us gentle and so mild
Some are pure of heart, and happy in their confusion
Others unctuously approach to indoctrinate the child
Close your mind to science - accept the creationists' illusion
Yes, god loves us all and yet, so strange to tell
He has a plan for sinners — they burn for ever in hell
Where is forgiveness — when remorse is good and true
Explain God's penchant for sacrifice - the biblical barbecue
Do clerics believe what they say they believe
Are Israel and Palestine going to fight to the death
Am l the only one 'in step' amongst this religious illusion
Think for yourself - form a logical conclusion
Religion, this strange enigmatic unproven philosophy
Brought about by those who wish to control the human psyche
Taught by those who claim to be empowered by god
Taught by those who rule with a vicious iron rod
Open your mind, study science - and god
Read the bible — read physics - how old is the world?
Ask questions, use logic, the world is your oyster
Don't let you mind be confined to a cloister

Gerald Mason

Penthusiasm

ARNOLD'S ARK

Arnold died just before Christmas so with all the festive excitement, it was well into January before Eva was able to make the visit. She had been secretly planning the trip for years, so when she pulled up outside the RSPCA sanctuary for the first time, she felt no anxiety, just excitement.

Following the kennelmaid down the passageway towards the dog block, she was almost overwhelmed by the stench which grew steadily more powerful, the closer they got. Wiping her eyes and holding her hanky over her nose made little difference.

'They're mucking out the runs; it's not usually this bad,' the green clad figure explained and Eva was glad she'd worn her old walking shoes with their thick cleated soles. 'There's a label on the front of each cage that will give you all the details about each dog: age, breed, name, personality and so on. Though generally speaking, you can tell what they're like from how they behave towards visitors. I'll leave you to have a wander round on your own – just come back to the desk if you see one you like. Then we can do the paperwork.'

Eva had been wanting a dog for as long as she could remember. Arnold had a whole book of reasons why a dog would be wrong for them, so every time she suggested getting one, he had a response already prepared, so eventually, she'd stopped asking.

The number and variety of dogs on offer was almost overwhelming. Eva walked straight past the small yappy ones with Arnold's voice ringing in her ears 'think of the area – a barking dog lowers the value of properties and the Residents Association just wouldn't stand for it.' She lingered in front of several big hairy hounds until Arnold's voice reminded her, 'Just think of the hairs on the carpets, you'll never get rid of the smell of damp dog and what would Mrs Wellbelow have to say?' Eva shook her head to get rid of the voice. She'd dealt with the Mrs Wellbelow problem by giving the cleaning lady notice straight after Arnold died. Having a cleaner had been his idea and Eva had felt ineffective enough without her constant criticism. It also meant she would have extra money; Arnold had insisted she paid the cleaner out of the housekeeping money, reducing what he liked to describe as a generous amount to a level that had made it hard to make ends meet and still provide him with a level of indulgence he considered appropriate for his status in her father's company.

The kennel maid caught up with Eva as she reached the last kennel.

'Find anything you fancy?'

'Not really,' said Eva. 'I don't know quite what I want, but I didn't find it.'

'Tell you what, why don't we do all the paperwork, get your home check done and then you can come back again. We've got another load of dogs in the assessment unit. They will be ready for re-homing by the end of the week. I'll do the home visit on Wednesday and then you can have first pick of the new dogs on Friday morning.'

Eva was pleased to find that her house met all the RSPCA's requirements and that she too passed muster, even though she'd never owned a dog before. Having bought everything on the list given to her by Jenny, the kennel maid, she was first into the centre's car park on Friday morning.

Prepared for the smell, it didn't seem quite as overpowering as it had been on her first visit. There were no empty kennels that morning and deliberately refusing to listen to Arnold's voice, she walked up and down the concrete paths until she found just the dog she had always dreamt of. A delicate-looking beagle stood forlornly in the corner of her run and as Eva bent to read the card, a silky head pushed against her hand. *This is Beaker. She is a spayed female beagle about two years old.*

Eva raced back to Jenny at the reception desk.

'I've found the dog I want. Quick, before anyone else sees her. She's the one. Please can I have her?'

'Are you sure? I don't know much about her, she was transferred here from our Cambridge branch. Beagles can be difficult, you know. I don't even know if this one is house-trained.'

Penthusiasm

'I am absolutely positive that she's the dog for me. She looks intelligent and I'm sure she'll be a quick learner. I've already found a dog training class with spaces and I got everything on the list you gave me. I've even brought the lead with me ready. Please.'

Eva signed the papers, paid her money and collected Beaker from the kennel. As they left the RSPCA centre, the little dog stayed close by her side. She trembled as Eva lifted her into the car and whimpered quietly on the journey home.

Over the next few months, Beaker became everything that Eva wanted in a dog. She was obedient and intelligent, but kept her spirit of independence and would tease Eva if they were at home in the safety of the house or garden. When they were out, Beaker stayed close to her mistress, always alert for possible danger. Together they attended 'socialisation' classes, passed basic training with flying colours and then graduated to agility training. Beaker was happy to be the first over the A frame or down the tunnel, as long as Eva was waiting for her at the other end.

It was late one Saturday afternoon and they were still in the park when Eva became aware of a man watching them from a stand of trees. She had an uncomfortable feeling that she'd seen him before. Calling the dog to her, she clipped on the lead and left for home. Once indoors, she convinced herself that she had been victim of an overactive imagination. Why would anyone be stalking her? Determined not to be spooked, Eva took Beaker to the park again the following afternoon but just in case, they left the house straight after lunch. The park was beginning to fill up with families making the most of the fine weekend. Beaker was good with children so she fondled her head and let her off the lead for a run. It was only as Beaker set off, that Eva noticed the man, once again standing alone amongst the trees.

'Beaker,' she called, making her voice as sharp as she could. 'Come here.' For once, Beaker ignored her command and set off towards the trees. Ignoring her anxiety, Eva set off after the dog and was amazed to see Beaker greet the man like a long-lost friend. He tickled the dog behind her ears, patted her sides and rubbed the proffered tummy as the dog rolled on the ground in ecstasy. Eva was amazed. Was this really the serious little dog that rarely strayed from her side and more to the point, who was the man?

Looking up from where he was kneeling, the man stuck out a muddy hand.

'Hello. My name is Ryan. You must be Beaker's new owner. It's marvellous to see her again.'

'How do you know Beaker and how did you find us?'

'Please come and have tea with me and give me a chance to explain. You don't need to be frightened – the café will be busy, plenty of people around and we can sit outside.'

For once, Eva didn't stop to weigh up her options; she put her trust in Beaker and followed the man. With a pot of tea on the metal table between them, Ryan began his explanation.

'Please keep what I tell you to yourself. I could get into trouble and lose my job if any one finds out what I've done.' Eva nodded and Ryan continued. 'I work in a research facility just outside Cambridge – I'm a tech in the animal lab. The company is gradually reducing the number of live animals they use for trials...'

'But surely that's a good thing,' Eva interrupted.

'True, but the problem is, they destroy the animals they no longer need. Beaker was one of my favourites and was on the list to be terminated; so I smuggled her out. I took her to the RSPCA and told them I'd found her straying on the M11.'

'But how did she get here?' asked Eva.

'The RSPCA in Cambridge re-homed her but the man who took her was unkind, so I lured her away and brought her to the RSPCA here. My brother-in-law lives near here, and I've been coming down most weekends to keep watch until I was sure you were ok.'

'I hope you consider me fit to look after Beaker, but how did you find us? Did you hack into their computer?'

'No, nothing like that. I chipped her with a GPS, so I can

Penthusiasm

tell where she is – and incidentally you are everything I'd hoped for Beaker.'

'Well, thanks for that,' said Eva. 'Seriously though, you are most welcome to come and visit Beaker any time you like.'

Once they had finished their tea, Eva and Ryan took Beaker for the rest of her walk. By the time they left to go their separate ways, they had agreed to meet again the following weekend and already felt a bond.

Several weeks later, and after a lot of consideration, Eva asked Ryan a question:

'Are there any more like Beaker in your lab? I've made lots of friends at agility classes and my friend Sharon is looking for a new dog. She and her partner just split up, and he took the dog. She loves Beaker and handles her really well. I know it's not legal and it could get you into trouble; but could you get a dog for Sharon? I haven't said anything to her, just in case you can't, but is it possible?'

'There are still fifteen beagles left in the lab. As I told you before, as soon as they finish their bit of the trial, they are tagged for destruction. Beaker's littermate Bunsen is due to finish her trial at the end of next week. I'm sure I could get her out and I'm willing to give it a go. Sort it out with Sharon and give me a ring before Wednesday.'

Sharon was pleased to hear she had a chance to provide a home for Bunsen, so Eva arranged for Ryan to bring the dog to her house on Saturday morning. All went smoothly and in no time, Sharon and Bunsen had completed socialisation and basic training and joined Eva and Beaker in agility classes. News spread slowly but secretly, that Eva could find dogs for caring owners, so at regular intervals, Ryan would bring an ex-trial dog to Eva for re-homing. All went well until they reached number seven; Petrie was identified by the lab for destruction and Eva had arranged a new home. The evening Ryan tried to smuggle the dog out, the alarms went off and he was marched to the Managing Director's office by two armed guards. After a difficult interview, the managing director allowed Ryan to keep the dog and, in return for not contacting the press, agreed not to prosecute but couldn't be persuaded to allow Ryan to keep his job.

Once Eva had re-homed Petrie and feeling guilty for getting Ryan sacked, they discussed the future.

'I'm sorry I got you fired. What are you going to do now?'

'I don't know. My brother suggested I should move down here – he reckoned there might be a better chance of a job down this way but I think he's just trying to get me away from the lab in case they change their minds and involve the police.'

'I've been thinking something over for quite a while now. Arnold's life insurance has finally paid out and if I sell the house, I should have enough money to buy a kennels. There's one up for sale towards the coast. If I get it, would you come and work with me? We could provide boarding and training classes as well as a home for some more beagles. I know you agreed not to contact the press – but I didn't. If I go to the lab, maybe I could persuade them to let me have all the remaining beagles in return for not contacting the media. I could be quite reasonable and let them finish the trial first. It'd even save them the cost of destroying and disposing of the dogs. What do you reckon?'

'Sounds like a plan – it would be marvellous; if you can pull it off.'

The project took much longer to complete than to plan. The lab were surprisingly co-operative. They agreed to gradually transfer the remaining beagles to Eva once their trials were completed. The kennels needed a lot of work, so she and Ryan and the beagles moved into a caravan, until the renovations were finally finished. Then, once the kennels were ready, Eva and Ryan organised an unofficial launch party for everyone who had helped bring her dream to life. They even sent an invitation to the lab's Managing Director and were amazed when he turned up.

'Welcome, everyone,' said Eva. 'We are so pleased that so many of you managed to get here today as we owe you all a big thank you; there's no way we could have got this far without your help.'

Penthusiasm

Eva waited for the applause to die down before she continued: 'There is one last thing to do before we can advertise and open to the public and that is to announce our name. We thought long and hard – we considered 'Beagles Retreat' and 'Dogs for Life' but in the end,' she added with a grin, 'we settled for simplicity. So - please will you all raise a glass of Dandelion and Burdock and drink a toast to Arnold's Ark.'

Anna Hitch

MORNING COMMUNION

The smell and throb of diesel
as the tractored plough
backcombs the gulls
from the furrowed field.
The soil's seductive sweetness
and the flanks of rounded earth
give fertile promise
demanding to be touched.
Grass filled with morning damp
yields flattened underfoot
in wait for the lifting sun
to disperse those misted clamps
ghost kissed among the dingles.
Eggs boiled, still
with feathers on the shell.
Bread warm in tablecloth
trails bacon-laden air.
Breakfast off the land
wife wafted on a smile.

Hugh Rose

Penthusiasm

WHICH WAY THE RAINBOW?

Arc of fine balance
embrace of pure harmony,
sun meeting raindrops,
since before Man began.
Red, Orange, Yellow,
then - Green, Blue and Indigo,
a brush stroke of Violet
and blending's complete.

Eternally magical
but fleeting,
unreachable,
in slowest dissolve
to ethereal fade.
Elusive translucence,
with nature's intransigence
gently withdraws pots of gold
from our dreams.

But...

What if Green clashed with Red,
Orange flared out at Indigo
Violet shuddered at Yellow,
leaving Blue to come last?

Spring arrived in September?
and all the rest had floods or ice,
What if heat scorched December?
excepting February, when roses now bloomed?

Nah! Set in stone, isn't it!
Global warming? A con that is!
What's a few polar bears?
Loads of rainforest left.

Seven Monmouthshire Writers

Won't be in my time,
and I love the sun anyway.
Making it up they are,
having a laugh!

So - tread lightly? Keep plundering?
Hear the juggernaut rumbling?

Action or dithering?
Eyes open ? Ears listening
to the relentless drip dripping.

as the clock goes on ticking
and the palette's repositioning?

Tic - toc
Tic - toc

Which way the rainbow?

Louise Longworth

Penthusiasm

CHILDHOOD MEMORIES

I was born in Jessops Women's Hospital, Sheffield just after the end of the Second World War (although you may be surprised to learn that is not *really* why the war ended).

Even though it was mid-March, my father had to dig deep snow away from the garage so that he could take his wife to hospital.

My mother had a relatively easy delivery because I was a very small baby, significantly underweight. Almost immediately I caught whatever was going round at the hospital at the time. Consequently, when my mother was considered well enough to go home a week later, as was normal in those days, I was kept behind. My mother was warned that her baby son might not survive the night.

I was more than a month-old before I beat the odds, and pneumonia, and made it to the family home in the Sheffield suburb of Millhouses, best known for its child-friendly park with a large stream-fed paddling pool. (Today this landmark is no more, killed no doubt by the Health & Safety Gestapo).

Home was a large, old semi, which my parents had bought shortly before I was born, to accommodate a growing family: me and my sister, Margaret – two years ahead of me in age and light years ahead in everything else – and our long-haired Welsh collie sheepdog called Ajo [*pronounced ah-yo*], an Eskimo name which my father had selected because of the dog's likeness to a husky.

Although Ajo didn't know it at the time, he was later to teach me to walk by being a handy mobile device for pulling oneself up with. On second thoughts, maybe he did know it because he was only *slightly* less intelligent than both my father, a brilliant research physicist and my mother, a clever mathematician, scientist and translator/linguist.

I wonder now whether my anxious mother paid too much attention to her miraculously recovered son because my sister, who had been the lone apple of her eye until then, apparently seemed to resent my presence. It was a feud which Margaret and I successfully managed to keep festering for more than a dozen years, well into our adolescence...

By the time I could walk, Margaret had perfected her technique: find out what the younger sibling was not supposed to do and quietly tell him to do it... 'Don't go off down that side path; you'll get stuck in the mud,' my mother might say to her sensible, obedient daughter. 'Go down that path there and see what you can find,' my sister would then tell her gullible, unruly toddler brother.

But it didn't take me too long to develop my own methods for making trouble in return. I know this because many years later, as two now very devoted adults, my sister and I each have a similar, sneaking guilty feeling that we were the main aggressor.

Actually, my very early memories are entirely unreliable. Are they truly my memories or the mental cinecast of family anecdotes which have been circulating for years?

I think I really do remember the 'pig lady' who came to collect the kitchen waste and add it to the barrel of slops on the cart behind her horse.

But I certainly don't truly remember the time we lost the dog.

Apart from being a teaching aid, Ajo was also a trusted baby-sitter, the story goes. Our friends the Clarks, who lived quite a way up the road, were often given the task of looking after the two of us along with their own three girls. Ajo came with us, too, perhaps to make sure that when the four girls ganged up on me, the only boy, I didn't lose too much blood!

On one particular occasion, my mother went to collect us, completely forgetting the canine childminder who was happily playing with the Clark children. Several hours later Mr Clark rang my father to tell him that our dog was still at their house.

'Bring him to the phone,' my father suggested. When handset was to dog's ear, he said: 'Ajo, come home,' and the trusty guardian arrived back in minutes.

Penthusiasm

And I wonder if I also remember the fact that Ajo would dart out of the house a full ten minutes before my father arrived home from work. Apparently our family pet would meet the car about a mile away down on the main road and run alongside it, in and out of the traffic, until they both got home.

Ah, well! Memories. Best not get me started.

Steve Hoselitz

Seven Monmouthshire Writers

BUCKET LIST

Eileen Arthur was 85 when she sold the family home and moved lock, stock and a few bits of furniture into a small, ground floor flat in the city.

'I don't want to live in a retirement complex with a load of other oldies,' she explained to her son. 'There's stuff I still want to do and don't worry, I'll be close enough if either of us has a crisis.'

Once she was settled and comfortable in her new home with its tiny back yard and minimalist interior, she considered her circumstances. She reckoned that she had about five years left, so she set about drawing up two lists. The first itemised those things she was going to waste as little time as possible doing. It included housework, which was why she had chosen a tiny place with tiled floors, no stairs and minimal furniture and she had already developed a technique of cleaning the wet room by pirouetting with the showerhead in one hand and the Mr Muscle in the other. Gardening was next on the list. A small paved area to sit on and a few tubs for colour. No more mowing or weeding. A quick spray with the hose occasionally and she could replace the tubs each year… if she felt inclined. Cooking was the final item on the list. She'd buy ready prepared vegetables and salads, no more cake or jam making and she would THROW AWAY LEFTOVERS.

Once she'd completed the 'what not to do' list, she set about compiling a bucket list of all those things she'd had neither the time, the money or the opportunity to do when she was young. She liked eating, so she included trying all the cafés, restaurants and take-aways within walking distance, though she ruled out any with a hygiene rating of less than two.

'I'm not ready to go just yet,' she told her son as she showed him her lists. 'There's still stuff I want to do.'

Then she added some culture.

'I'll visit all the museums and art galleries within the city

Penthusiasm

limits. I've got to get my money's worth out of my bus pass before the council decides it's one expense too many.'

She bought a season ticket to the arts centre and the local theatre, so she could watch every new show, film or event staged.

'I reckon that should keep me busy,' she said.

As the years passed, Eileen gradually added to the lists and ticked off all the things she achieved. She kept a log of all the shows she'd seen, the cuisine she'd sampled and the friends she'd made until finally, on the evening of her 91st birthday, she put one last tick on the list, climbed into bed and turned out the light.

Anna Hitch

Seven Monmouthshire Writers

THE DAY I GAVE A DINNER PARTY

I planned a dinner party,
to overflow with glitterati.
It really was the most eclectic mix.
Mozart sitting - humming,
Beside him Hank (that's Marvin) - strumming,
and Shakespeare - swapping notes with Brian Rix.

Queen Victoria, scowling,
Austen (Jane) with JK Rowling
The great Gershwin meeting S Rachmaninov.
A sudden fanfare – Cleopatra!
And another – Oh! Sinatra!
and Tracy Emin bends the ear of Vince Van Gogh.

Then there's dear old JM Barrie,
Discussing flying with Prince Harry,
Who says, 'You really need my brother Will, not me.'
See - there's Churchill - next to Marx,
But it's the Harpo one – what larks!
Then Gypsy Rose - with namesake – Harper Lee.

Fonteyn twirls in with Fred Astaire - then Nureyev with Ginger,
Oops! Ghandi following Enoch Powell,
Mother Theresa - Star of India.
Paddington with Superman,
The Scottish team with Princess Anne –
Dorian Gray – with Peter Pan!

At that I ditched the seating plan!

Louise Longworth

Penthusiasm

SECOND THOUGHTS

Wandering I found, as I meandered around
in a garden so brambly green,
a statue of Zeus but it wasn't much use
a hole gaped where a head should have been.

A fern dipped a frond into a foul smelling pond
which resembled the primeval swamp.
There's no one to care for an area where
ardent lovers with dreams used to romp.

But wait just a mo, it's not all doom and woe,
there are butterflies, frogs, birds and bees.
Wild flowers bloom and the rooks have got room
to build clever nests high up in the tall trees.

Honeysuckle grows with rambling rose
sending fragrance so pure and so sweet.
There is joy in the air and I linger there
as I sit on a moss covered seat.

Wandering I found, as I meandered around
in a garden so brambly green,
a state of neglect but I suspect
it's more lovely than it's ever been.

Hugh Rose

MY CORONATION DAY MEMORIES

My Coronation Day memories - taken from the viewpoint of a neighbour who invited us into their house....

1953

'Well I just 'ope it don't rain,' mumbled Mrs Green to herself, as she flicked the yellow duster lazily over the utility furniture. 'All those people coming in 'ere. Dunno why Bert opened his big mouf. Always the same he is. Wantin' to impress the neighbours,' she grumbled. 'Oh well, guess there ain't many round 'ere who's got a tellie. Just 'ope it don't rain.'

Mrs Green gazed at the 12 inch TV set in the far corner of the little room. Proudly standing there in its brown wooden cabinet. Waiting to please an audience.

'We may live in a council 'ouse, but my Bert and Jim 'ave worked 'ard for that. Right in time for Coronation Day too. I could 'ave flattened Bert. There he was over the garden fence "Come round, Betty won' mind. Yeah, bring the kids. Not every day we get the chance to watch a Coronation, eh?" he had bragged.

'Always the same, my Bert. All those people tramping over my best lino in the 'all. Well, it just betta not rain,' she thought lovingly, dusting the top of the TV cabinet yet again.

Margaret Payne

Penthusiasm

KEEPING SCORE

Edith Masterson paused to button her white cardigan, before she stepped through the French doors of the residents' lounge and out into the garden. The lawn was laid out before her like a vast snooker table, the old people dotted around like the balls after an amateur's wild break.

'Your mother's down by the stream,' said the care assistant, looking barely old enough to have left school. 'She's been looking forward to seeing you.'

Deliberately choosing the stone steps in preference to the newly installed ramp, Edith made her way carefully down onto the grass and headed for her mother at the far side of the garden – near the corner pocket; on her way past, she greeted the other residents.

'Hello, Mrs Peterson,' she yelled at the deaf old lady, shrivelled with age and swathed in a bright red blanket. One point for a red ball; the thought sprang unbidden into her mind.

'Oh hello, Mavis; how are Don and the boys?'

'Fine, thank you, Mrs Peterson.' She had long since given up trying to correct the old lady. Who Mavis and Don were, she had no idea, but clearly they had more than one son.

'Hello, Mr Gordon.' She stopped to gently shake hands with one of the very few old men in the care home. He spent his time sucking noisily on the empty pipe he'd given up smoking years before. His blanket was a brown tweed affair which matched his flat cap.

Mrs Harrison was next. Blind as a bat and daft as a brush, she was resplendent in yellow. How on earth they'd managed to match her blanket to her hair, teeth and skin, Edith had no idea.

'Is that you, Elizabeth?' she queried.

'No, Mrs Harrison, it's me, Edith – Mrs Snell's daughter.'

'Did you see my daughter Elizabeth as you came through the lounge, dear? She's coming to see me this afternoon, you know.'

'No, Mrs Harrison, but I expect she'll be here soon,' said Edith tactfully, though she knew that the daughter was herself 80 and had emigrated to Australia over 30 years ago. She could see that Miss Innes, a tiny old lady with wild white hair and dressed entirely in pink, was fast asleep in a wicker chair under the magnolia so she didn't stop but continued towards her mother.

'Hello, Mother. It's me, Edith. How are you doing?'

'I know it's you, Edith. I saw you coming down the garden, talking to all those daft old biddies on the way. I'm cold, tired and hungry. Push me back to the house – it's nearly time for tea.'

Edith released the brake on the wheel chair and began to push the old lady back up the path. Her mother had adopted widow's weeds when Edith's father had died almost fifty years ago. She had never really forgiven him for leaving her and she had become steadily more embittered and complaining as the years passed. Listening with just half an ear as her mother complained about the nurses, the food, the home and the weather, Edith lost track and her mind wandered. The house had been converted to a care home from a country mansion which, for many years, had been open to the public. She had been round it with her mother in the carefree days before she was widowed.

'Hello again, Edith,' said the young care assistant. 'Thank you for pushing your mother in, she really does like to be at the front of the queue for tea. Today, we are serving it in the...'

'I can see,' said Edith, giggling as she pushed her mother's chair into the billiard room. '20 - I scored 20 in a single break!'

'What are you muttering about?' snapped her mother, 'Laughing and talking rubbish –they'll be booking you a room here if you aren't very careful.'

'Yes mother,' said Edith. 'Now, would you like a nice slice of Battenberg or a fondant fancy?'

Anna Hitch

Penthusiasm

JUST A PEBBLE!

The smouldering heat of the afternoon beat down onto my already tanned skin. The blue, shimmering sea stretched out before me, and the warm, pebbled sand surrounded me. Amidst the warmth and sunshine, the beach looked battered and scarred. Rubbish filled the crevices of the rock pools. The huge broken tree trunks, twisted metal and tilted boulders looked out of place, strewn across the calm, gentle, lapping ocean.

I glanced across Polena beach and listened to the joyful noise of the Sri Lankan children, romping and splashing in the far corner of the cove. My hands sunk into the sand beneath me and I drew out a fairly large pebble. It felt smooth, silky and warm in my palm. It was grey in colour, encircled with glistening stripes of white.

'Just a pebble,' I thought, 'but what a story it could tell.'

Where had it come from? Had it originally been part of a huge boulder that had stood static in the crystal blue sea for a thousand years, rooted firmly, surveying the fishermen and the daily life of the village people? At the weekends, had it watched the endless trail of old dilapidated buses, vans and cars spew out their eager cargo of locals, to cook their food by the welcoming sea? Had it been part of a rock diving platform for the noisy, thin, wiry children who clambered over it, like the tiny crabs that sheltered in its cracks and crevices?

Until that day maybe. Until the 26th of December 2004, when the sea unexpectedly erupted like a giant sea serpent, bringing total chaos and immense sadness.

When enormous rocks and boulders shook from their foundations, and were tossed into the air, spurting a million chippings in every direction, their smooth, worn surfaces, damaged and misshapen forever.

'It's just a pebble,' I mused again.

Its silence wasn't a problem. The people here can tell their stories of that day. Of how the fishing boats were thrown into the air and splintered like matchsticks. How huge heavy boulders were tossed effortlessly into the waves and landed way back from the beach, destroying everything in its violent path.

Where these mutilated lumps of stone will now stay, probably until another catastrophe.

Margaret Payne

Penthusiasm

TALKING TO JIM

Shirley and George later disagreed over who made the first move but Shirley would always remember the first time she saw him. He was walking across the dining room, tall and smart with thick white hair, a dignified figure despite his limp and walking stick. Men are a rare species in this place, she reflected, and the few there are can usually be found asleep in chairs, mouths open, but she liked the look of this one. She'd been here for three months and felt bored and old. Her daughter Janice had persuaded her, with characteristic bluntness: 'You've had three falls since Christmas, you've got a plastic hip and two dodgy knees – a residential home will make things easy for you – no more worries.' And so Shirley had left her cosy bungalow and cherished garden, and moved to Sunnyvale, bringing just a few possessions to remind her of a previous life.

Three days after the first sighting, Shirley spotted George again – this time in the lounge after lunch, sitting in one of the identical winged chairs by the huge, soundless television and reading *The Times*. She settled herself in a chair close by and began to do her crossword. Then, minutes later:

'What's a nice girl like you doing in a place like this?'

George was standing close to her chair, smiling as he stooped to speak and leaning on his stick. She looked up into his mischievous blue eyes and felt an unfamiliar tremor of excitement. She noticed his red silk tie with matching handkerchief.

'Oh, just waiting for a nice man like you to come along.'

'Well, here I am - the answer to your dreams. May I join you?'

Shirley nodded, and for thirty minutes they talked non-stop, finding out about one another, their pasts, their physical ailments and sharing worries about how to stay alert in the suffocating, disinfected atmosphere of Sunnyvale. George had been resident for six months, following recovery from a stroke which had left his right side weakened, and spoke with the benefit of experience.

'You've got to keep yourself busy, ignore the rules and don't get stuck with bores who want to tell you their life story....several times over.'

Shirley chuckled. 'Well that's all very well but I'm not interested in the activities – I get so fed up, next thing I'll be one of the snoozers,' and she looked towards a large woman, slumped heavily in her chair and snoring with gusto.

'Oh, not the organised activities - you've got to make your own fun. What are you doing tomorrow night?'

Shirley didn't reply – she never had plans.

'Well, I've got two tickets for *Kiss Me Kate* at the Guildford Theatre – shall I see you at reception at say 6.30pm – then we'll have time for a drink before it starts.'

'But can we do that – are we allowed?'

'Just leave everything to me. I'll see you tomorrow - and wear your most glamorous frock.'

And then he was gone. Shirley eased herself out of the chair and walked, smiling, across the lounge. She felt light-headed and for once in no need of her stick.

Back in her room, she settled down for an afternoon chat with Jim and today she had something to tell him. As always he smiled at her from their golden wedding photo on the dressing table, nestling between a picture of Janice's doomed wedding and, on the other side, two grandsons.

'I think I've just been picked up, Jim – I hope you don't mind. You know how much I still miss you – but now you're not here to give me a cuddle and tell me you love me, I'm lonely. So you won't begrudge me a bit of fun – he seems like a gentleman and he's not been as lucky as us – divorced twenty years ago, no children, and even tried to meet women on his computer. We're going to the theatre – how long is it since I did that? You were never interested.'

The following evening, Shirley allowed plenty of time to get ready – dressing was a slow business these days. She'd chosen a blue silk two piece last worn for a niece's wedding and was pleased to see that it still fitted her slim shape. Her grey blonde hair was freshly washed and styled – thanks to a visit to Goldilocks, the Home hairdresser. A final touch – her

Penthusiasm

precious pearl necklace, the last gift from Jim – completed the outfit. Not sure about glamorous but I'm not bad for an old codger, she thought as she looked in the mirror.

*****

After *Kiss Me Kate,* Shirley and George spent more time together. They shared a table at lunch and there were outings - to galleries, restaurants and even a tea dance. One night about six weeks after their first meeting, George walked her back to her room. At the door, he paused for a moment, looking serious.

'Shirley … I want you to know how happy you make me – I'm very fond of you, you know.'

And he slipped his arms around her waist, pulling her towards him; she could feel his lips against her cheek and there was a pleasing smell of aftershave. Shirley placed her hands in the small of his back and remained quite still, enjoying the pleasure of this closeness, letting the sensations run through her body as he held her.

Finally, as they drew apart, he said softly: 'Good night, my dear – sweet dreams.'

Next day was Janice's weekly visit – always the same – lunch at Sunnyvale and then a cream tea in a village nearby. 'It's good to get you out – you need a bit of fresh air,' Janice would say.

Janice was just finishing her second scone in the Copper Kettle when Shirley broke the news.

'I think I may be in love. I've met this sweet man called George and we get on ever so well…..I feel alive for the first time since your father died.'

'You mean you've made a nice friend?' Janice was trying to keep calm.

'No I mean love – I've got feelings for him.'

'I'm sorry, Mum, but you are eighty two years old and living in a retirement home – not a twenty year old in a Mills & Boon novel.'

'I don't want to fall out but I wanted you to know because things might develop…'

'Develop? What do you mean develop? Are you planning to elope? – just remember to pack the zimmer frames, won't you?'

'You've become very bitter since your divorce, Janice. I thought you'd be pleased for me.'

Shirley adopted the hurt look she often used when dealing with her domineering daughter.

'But I'm only thinking of you – I want to save you from making a bloody fool of yourself with a man you hardly know. I don't want things to end badly, you're so sensitive.'

Later after Janice had left for Hampshire, Shirley sat in her room alone and in silence – she wasn't in the mood to talk to Jim. Maybe I *am* being an old fool but I know how I feel – he makes me happy, as if I'm still attractive. It's different to Jim – there's a bit of danger in it – but maybe Janice is right and at my age I can't expect anything but bingo and knitting. She turned on the television, avoiding Jim's gaze, and soon fell asleep watching *Escape to the Country*.

*****

'She was very cutting, George, said we were too old for love and I couldn't expect any future in it.'

Shirley was sharing Janice's verdict with George over lunch the next day.

George looked down into the thin minestrone soup and moved his spoon slowly around the bowl. 'Well, what exactly did you say to her ... about the future?'

'Just how much I cared for you and that things might develop.'

He looked up quickly, his face bore a puzzled expression and his blue eyes were lacking their usual twinkle. 'We mustn't rush things, Shirley – we've been having a lovely time but we haven't known each other long.'

Shirley felt flushed, as if she'd been caught doing something wrong. 'I understand that, George, but we do have something special, don't we?'

'Of course my dear one.' He placed the spoon in the bowl

Penthusiasm

and moved his hand to cover hers. 'You know how important you are to me.'

And then he got up from his chair. 'I'm sorry but I must be going now, I've got a game of bridge in ten minutes.'

'But you haven't finished your lunch......'

As he rose, Shirley noticed a thin dribble of soup on the front of his shirt, and the handkerchief protruding from his breast pocket was frayed.

Over the next few weeks, Shirley saw less of George. He explained that he had some family business to take care of, but when they met, he was his usual charming self and Shirley told herself that all was well.

One Friday morning after breakfast, the April sunshine was finding its way into the gloom of Sunnyvale and Shirley decided to have coffee in the sun lounge. This was a room she liked, with its large windows, wooden floor and cheerful yellow and green seating – you could breathe in there, unlike the rest of the home. She looked around for a free chair and was surprised to see George seated at the far end of the room with his back towards her. As she walked over to greet him, she noticed that he was not alone. Next to him, she recognised the flushed face of Brenda Flowers, a new resident, noted for her dyed red hair and overdone make-up. Shirley was about to call out when suddenly and shockingly she realised that George's hand was resting comfortably on Brenda's knee.

It was too late, Brenda had seen her.

'Shirley - how are you? Come and join us for coffee.'

As she spoke, the familiar hand was swiftly withdrawn from Brenda's knee and George turned round to face Shirley.

'No, thank you, I'm just after a magazine to read.'

She turned and headed towards the door where George caught up with her.

'It wasn't what you think – I was just trying to comfort her – she's feeling lonely.'

'Of course, George, whatever you say, now I must be getting on.' Her voice sounded stronger than she felt and she pushed past him.

Back in her room, Jim was waiting as she slumped into her chair.

'I've made such a fool of myself. I've had a fling and now I've been jilted, by a geriatric gigolo......how could I? I've no experience of this sort of thing - you were the only man in my life - what am I supposed to do.' She stared hopelessly at Jim's photograph, knowing that he had no answers for her - she was on her own now and he couldn't help her. Gently, she picked up the frame, gave Jim a soft kiss and laid him down on the table.

She sat quietly for some time and gradually felt her mood lighten as she smiled to herself – *Well, a love affair at my age – maybe I'm not ready for the scrap heap – there may be some life left in the old girl yet, you never know.* On the table next to her, she saw a notice for an opera trip the following week. *I've never been to an opera,* she thought, *maybe I'll try it – why do I always need a man to get me doing things – you never know, I might have some fun.*

Maggie Harkness

Penthusiasm

NO TITLE

A sacred vow, an act of love
To treasure more than life itself
One's promise to another for evermore
Until temptation knocks at the half closed door

D'you love me, dear - of course I do
And in her heart it's true
But Eden fruit is far too sweet
He'll not find out - I'll be discreet

A liaison here - a liaison there
In smart hotels in the afternoon
Life at home becomes a bore
Temptation beckons through the half closed door

Her sense of values cast aside
She lives for the moment - hell bent on pleasure
Fast cars and whiskey - money and clothes
Cocaine, gambling - anything goes

Surrounded by admirers - predatory males
Their demands are quite simple, it's sex that they want
She's passed from one to another - till they've all had their fill
Remove sex and she's nothing - intellectually nil

Time marches on - she's no longer young
Invitations are few and the phone doesn't ring
She drinks far too much - to steady her nerves
Her thickening body no longer boasts curves

Where are they now? These 'one time' admirers
They've moved on - she's rejected - like a faulty component
They are fickle, self centred, deceitful and shallow
She's paid the ultimate price for a life without value

Gerald Mason

Seven Monmouthshire Writers

BEST WISHES FOR THE 21ST CENTURY

(Inspired by 'An Irish Blessing')

May your Guinness slip down smoothly, in the company of true friends,
May your soul be sure to find its mate -
and the devil miss the wedding announcement!
May you perceive the stars in a sodium-free sky, and your world be forever green,
yet free from envy.
May your Premium Bond fight its way to the top, but may you never have to.
May your family tree grow many branches, and may you see it bear sweet fruit.
May you wake up and find the Income Tax demand was just a dream,
and the overdraft - just a computer error.
May you always have a fine inquisitiveness about your fellow man,
but never judge him without first putting your feet in his Doc Martens.
May you, and your kettle always whistle
and you and yours stay always right in tune.
May you feel soft rain upon your face,
but never through holes in your boots!
May your heart and your mind be as open as your door,
and may all your finest dreams be waking.
Whenever you visit your doctor, may all your symptoms turn out fine,
but -
when you are finally ready for the stairway to heaven?
May the Devil's escalator be on the blink!

Louise Longworth

Penthusiasm

BORDER FORCE CHRISTMAS...

'It's like this, guv. There is new rules which 'ave come into effect this year so I can't just let you in like what I've done in the past.

'I'm sorry but me job's on the line and me and the missus are struggling to make ends meet, even though we both got work. JAM they calls it – just about managing. I calls it Titanic – bloody well sinking...

'You can come in if you've got the new BOVVA – UK Borders One-week Visitors' Visa. They may not 'ave 'em available yet where you come from: I'm getting that all the time from you foreign chappies... we was supposed to be prepared for Brexit but somehow details got overlooked. You'll have to get one from the kiosk over there. Just fifty quid. Nah! We don't take Euros. Just Sterling and Dollars.

'I'm afraid your staff – them little helpers you've got wiv yer – will probably not get in now. I don't know where they come from, but they're very small and so they're going to 'ave to 'ave a dental check. I expect they're what we calls 'unaccompanied minors'. If they is, they'll have to go to one of our clearing centres, but the one in Calais was closed over a year ago so basically, mate, they're going be turned away. Poor little 'fings. Still, what can I do about it? Nuffink!

'Now 'em animals you've got are also going to be a big problem this time. I know we've let 'em through in the past - when we was in Europe - but all that's changed now. Your lot don't allow us to take our pets abroad any more so now you need a special permit from one of our foreign embassies to bring 'em 'ere, and they're not issuing any more this year 'cause it's part of a quota system. Sorry, mate, that's just how it is... You'll have to pull that sled yourself. Big chap like you should manage...

'Now, let's just look at what you've got on board, shall we? Fsssth! Cor, you'll be lucky. They'll all need to be unwrapped in the shed over there. We've had new scanners on order all year but they're made in Germany and we've had a bit of a falling out with 'em, know what I mean? So it's back to the sorting shed. 'Ere's a little tip, try to get Nicola, short hair, Scottish accent... She'll give you an easier time with duty payable than some of the others. If you get one of the other blokes, they might charge you top whack. If you can't get Scotty, try slipping one of the blokes a back 'ander... They used to be pretty straight but nowadays it's everyone for 'emselves 'ere.

'An 'ere's a tip fer nuffin... Lose the red suit and that beard. Else people might take you for Jeremy bleedin Corbyn. Know what I mean?

'OK, Mate... Over to the kiosk now. Don't be long. I know I'm on nights but it's December 24th and I want to knock off soon...'

Steve Hoselitz

Penthusiasm

THE PROBLEM

The problem keeps jabbing
like a splinter in a finger
always in a position
that two thumbs can't squeeze.
It can be ignored until
something is grasped
whereupon
it gives a reminder, viciously
that it hasn't gone.
In the end,
what should have been done
in the beginning,
a needle is used
to rend and sting
the flesh
causing more damage than
the splinter until
with a joyous spurt
which feels like triumph
it emerges – insignificant
not worth the hurt or bother
as the wound soon heals.

Hugh Rose

OLLIE AND MOLLIE

Ollie and Mollie were dancers, who felt worn out and jaded, and so
were relieved to be due a vacation - but then couldn't decide where to go.
So they climbed on a steam train, exhausted, not caring a jot where it went,
but the rumble and bumble of 'train-speak' worked its magic before they reached Kent!

The toe-tapping started in Taplow –
got them 'Waltzing' in Walsingham too,
They 'Cha-Cha' 'd to Chatham and 'Tap-dance' 'd through Thatcham,
(took a bathroom break when they reached Looe.)

Next they 'Salsa' 'd in Salisbury - did the 'Foxtrot' in Folkestone,
after that the itinerary went crazy,
for they danced a minuet, in the wilds of Tibet!
What happened to just being lazy?

They 'Hustle' 'd to Brussels – 'Shimmy' 'd on to Sri Lanka,
'Polka' 'd round Poland 'til late.
'Rocked' in Bangkok- in fact – 'Rocked - Round – The - Clock,'
but – 'American-Smoothed' New York State.

They 'Jived' in Jaipur - Namur (and Dartmoor!)
In Russia they learned the 'Kalinka'
On the good ship *Endeavour* they had the best dance fun ever,
when they Horn-pipe' 'd on board - fit to sink her!

They 'Freaked out in 'Frisco, with disco-m-bobulating 'Disco'
In Jakarta they dabbled in 'Jazz'.

Penthusiasm

They 'Arab-esque'd on to Egypt, where they 'Burlesque'd and 'Heel-flipped'.
Next to Rio, for 'Razzamataz'!

Tanganika got 'Tango'; 'Fandango' and 'Mambo',
In Seville (as you'd guess!) 'twas 'Flamenco'.
They 'Can-Can' 'd through Paris - 'Highland Flung' all round Harris,
'Soft- Shoe- Shuffle' went - where? . . . ' Off to Buffalo!'

Sabbatical over, they've disembarked in Dover, 'cos they rejoin the ballet today,
So – let's hear it for dancers - who bust a gut to entrance us.
All together now . . .

'Hip-Hop' - Hooray!

Louise Longworth

BEFORE CHRISTMAS

From the diary of Bernard, recently relocated to Missoula, Montana, USA

Wednesday November 23rd
More snow this morning. Dorothy next door says it started back in October, about a week earlier than normal, which means a hard winter. I wonder if she's right. I love snow.

She invited Glenys and me in for cherry pie and coffee. We've only been here since Monday but she's already been so nice. I'm glad we're here and not back in Milton Keynes. We hardly knew our neighbours there. Earl, her husband, works for a local car dealership. And it's something called Thanksgiving tomorrow. All her family are coming – she called them her folks. I said they could park in our drive; she says it's a drive*way*.

Thanksgiving: Thursday November 24th
I love snow. That's partly why we moved here, and of course to be near our daughter, Gail who's expecting her first. Chuck, our son-in-law, has a good a job here in Missoula. I haven't really gathered exactly what he does, but whatever it is, Gail says he's doing really well.

About six inches of snow fell overnight and I spent the morning shovelling the driveway and I also cleared the pavement outside – I suppose I should call it the sidewalk now. At about lunchtime a big street maintenance truck came along and blew snow off the road and onto the sidewalk and across the end of the driveway – I had to clear it again so that Dorothy's folks could park. I wonder if it'll snow again tonight.

Friday November 25th
Exactly a month to go before Christmas and I spent the morning shovelling overnight snow from the driveway. I left the sidewalk in case the truck came past again but it didn't. Dorothy came round to say thank you for allowing people to

Penthusiasm

park on our driveway. She seemed surprised at the small car we have and suggested that we talk to Earl about trading it in for something bigger. They're so nice.

Saturday November 26th
Great, still more snow. It is our first weekend here in Montana near our daughter. Such fun. I'm glad we sold up and moved out here. We're never going back! After I had cleared the driveway and the sidewalk, I put on skis and slid into town. It only took me half an hour – and only twice as long to get back. When I got home Glenys said there was something wrong with the heating. It appears the boiler isn't working: they call it a 'furnace' here. I asked Dorothy who could help and she told me Earl's cousin would call round later. They're so nice here. The snow truck came and blew the snow back on the driveway. Apparently they come every other day. I wish I'd known...

Later Earl's cousin, Dean, came round to look at the furnace, even though it's Saturday. I made a joke about 'Earl and Dean' but no one laughed. Maybe they didn't have Pearl & Dean out here. He said he could mend it but it might be better to buy a new one. He says the modern ones are more efficient. He also suggested that we might want to buy a different car: he's the second person to have mentioned it.

Sunday November 27th
It seems that it snows most nights here through (or should I say thro) the winter – and sometimes in the day, too. I cleared the driveway and the sidewalk – no snow truck today: there you go! I've got the hang of it now.

Glenys and I wanted to go into town to meet Gail, our daughter, but the car wouldn't start after I had dug it out of the snowdrift. It doesn't seem to like the cold! Glenys rang Gail and rearranged our get-together for tomorrow.

Later the snow truck came past and blew snow off the road and over the driveway. I must remember tomorrow to ask Dorothy why it came today!

Seven Monmouthshire Writers

Monday November 28th
Dean called round to fit the new furnace. They do things so quickly here and without any fuss. It seems we've got the first of a brand new model which has just come out and is a lot bigger than we really need, but because it's new, it's on offer and we've got it at the same price as a smaller one. Dean is thoughtful. Everyone seems to like our accent here though they do confuse us with the Australians. When I told Dean that Glenys came from Wales, he was even more confused.

I remembered to ask Dorothy why the snow truck had come round yesterday and she said it was because it was the Sunday after Thanksgiving. I wish I'd known. Later I shovelled about 8in of fresh snow off the driveway and tried to open the garage door to put the car inside but it was frozen closed. I didn't manage to start the car... Glenys rang Gail to tell her we couldn't make it into town today either.

Tuesday November 29th
It was sixteen below last night. The new furnace isn't working too well and we are very cold. I rang Dean first thing this morning and asked him to come round. He said he'd try. There was no snow overnight but it's really icy now and the sidewalk is treacherous. Dorothy invited us in for coffee when she learned that our heating wasn't working well. She says Dean is a bit of a cowboy, much like the rest of Earl's 'kin' as she called them. We can't get the car out because the snow that the truck blew across the end of the driveway is now frozen solid. Anyway the car still doesn't seem to want to start, so we couldn't drive in to town anyway. Glenys rang Gail again to explain. She said not to worry, she'd come to see us.

Later, after seeing me struggling with the icy blockage at the end of the driveway Dorothy suggested that instead of digging snow with a shovel, I should buy a 'motorized pedestrian snow blower'. Her cousin, Danny, sells them at a good price. We're lucky to have such a nice 'neighbor'.

Penthusiasm

Thursday December 1st
A new month and more than a foot of new snow has fallen in two days. Lovely.

I didn't write my diary yesterday. It was not a day to remember. I tried to ring Dean but there was no answer. We were too cold to do much and I couldn't start the car.

Today things are looking up. Danny came round with a snow blower. He's so helpful. It's a great bit of kit! And he helped me open the frozen garage door so that we could put it away safely. Unfortunately that means we can't put the car away but it doesn't really matter because I haven't been doing that anyway.

Fortunately we have plenty of food in the wonderful two-door fridge we got with the house. Gail came round here for coffee. She suggested that we should get someone else to fix the heating. She doesn't seem to think Dean is up to the job. Perhaps I shouldn't say this because she's our daughter, but she's *so nice*. She said we should trade in the car for a 4x4: everyone has them round here apparently. I'll talk to Earl about it tomorrow.

There's fresh snow falling now. Great! I can use the new blower in the morning.

Friday December 2nd
I was trying to open the frozen garage door to get out the snow blower when Dean came round to look at our heating. He said that it needed different fuel to work efficiently. He made some adjustments and said it should now work. Glenys and I are getting warm again after three cold nights!

I wanted to talk to Earl about changing the car for a 4x4 but they're not home next door. Glenys wonders if they've gone away for the weekend. Dorothy did say something about a cabin in the woods but I wasn't paying full attention.

Saturday December 3rd
The sun came out today and the temperature rose a little. There are icicles everywhere. We both went out into the garden – I can't get used to calling it a yard. That's how we

met our neighbours on the other side for the first time. They seem so nice too, like everyone out here. They had been away. They introduced themselves as Connie and Clyde. I said it sounded like Bonnie and Clyde but no one laughed. Clyde helped me get the snow blower out of the garage but we couldn't start it. He said the cheap Chinese engines were not much good in the cold. I said my car was like that too, but it was American. He didn't laugh.

Sunday December 4th
More snow today, on top of the ice. Made things very slippery. Glenys went down with a crack. Earl, who'd come back on his own from their cabin in the Blackfoot Valley, asked if she'd hurt her fanny. I thought he was being very vulgar until it was explained to me that he meant her backside. We couldn't get the snow blower going, nor the car. He said that Dorothy's cousin, Danny, was a bit of a cowboy and that all her kin were a bit rough.

Monday, December 5th
Bright but cold today. Several degrees below. I wanted to talk to Earl about changing the car but he'd gone to work early, I presume, and Dorothy was still not home. Strange that. She'd normally been around most of the time.
   Glenys rang Gail for a chat but we can't meet up at present 'til I can get the snow-blower going again and the car started. Still, we can walk to the local Mall in a few minutes, so we're not short of food and we're going out for a pizza tonight.

Tuesday December 6th
We bumped into Earl at the pizza parlour last night. They only do take-outs so Earl came and had his pizza with us. Dorothy is still away but he didn't seem to want to talk about it. He said he'd be happy to sell me a car and I should pop in to his dealership today. He told me not to worry about my present 'vee-hickle' because he'd seen it in our driveway so he knew what it was worth. Helpful as usual. A little more snow today. Still very cold and now the furnace is playing up again.

Penthusiasm

Thursday, December 8th
Our new car – or should I say truck – arrived today. A Dodge Ram Laramie. Earl says it was almost new and 'the best bargain on the lot'. I quipped that it seemed to cost a 'lot' but no one laughed. The garage sent a man to tow away our old car. The tow truck made short shrift of the snow and ice on our driveway. That's a relief. The driver was so nice. Dean came round and fiddled with the furnace. I don't know what he does in there, but after he'd been, it was working again: such a relief.

Saturday, December 10th
We were due to drive into town today to meet Gail for coffee, but the heating is playing up again so I needed to stay in for Dean. Glenys won't drive over here. She's never driven on the right side of the road – she calls it the wrong side - or an automatic and she hates the big Ram truck. We said we'd now meet Gail tomorrow downtown.

Dean did something to the furnace and said it should be OK now.

I couldn't get the snow blower working but I did manage to clear the end of the drive by shovelling. I now leave snow clearing until later in the day in case the snow truck drives past.

Sunday, December 11th
We took a cab into town to meet Gail. I should have thought of that before! I don't really like driving the Dodge either – it's way too big. Anyway the snow-plough was round again and blocked the end of the driveway. Must have been clearing the road during the night! We left Dean in the house mending the furnace. When we got home, he'd got it working again. Said the filter was clogged. Helpful and nice.

Monday, December 12th
The heating went off just after Dean left. I couldn't get him on his cell-phone. The cold kept us awake during the night, but

perhaps it was just as well since it meant we saw the police car outside Dorothy's house at about 3 am. No sign of Dorothy but Earl went off with the police. Later a policeman, Officer Krupczyk, called at our house. (*Catsick* I called him but no one laughed). He was so nice. Asked a lot of questions but I'm afraid we couldn't give him much help. He wondered why our house was so cold. I told him about the furnace and how helpful Dean had been. He noticed the Dodge Ram as he was leaving and asked me about something called out-of-state vehicle registration. I said I'd talk to Earl about it and he just laughed.

Tuesday, December 13th
Gail called round unexpectedly this morning. She'd heard some local gossip and wanted to see if we were OK? She wouldn't say what the gossip was but it had really spooked her. I showed her the Dodge and she said it was too big for us. That's what Glenys thinks too. Women! Still, she admired the driveway. Said it was the clearest she'd seen in Missoula. I felt so proud. Later Dean rang. Said he'd heard we were still having trouble with the furnace. Helpful as always, he said he'd see what he could do.

Wednesday December 14th
Dean called to look at the furnace. He said there's a well-known problem with unreliable fuel supply in our area. Seems that this could be the problem. Dean said he'd change the filter which could be clogged again.

I also managed to get the snow blower working properly. Danny had thought it was his two-stroke model and had filled it with the wrong fuel. It can happen so easily. Now after cleaning the fuel system and renewing the spark plug, it starts on the sixth or seventh pull without fail, which is just as well because there's heavy snow forecast tonight.

Saturday December 17th
The last weekend before Christmas and we finally managed to get out of the house today.

Penthusiasm

We've been snowbound for three days. I couldn't get the garage open to use the snow blower until this morning. I'd have used the car but on Thursday Officer 'Catsick' came back to tell me that there was some problem with the Ram's paperwork and I'd better not use it for now. Nice and helpful, like the others. We're hoping that we can go round to have Christmas dinner with Gail and Chuck. Chuck's parents will be there over Christmas, too. We have never met them but they sound nice.

Sunday December 18th
I wonder when Dorothy and Earl will be back home. I miss them both. Earl hasn't been around for a few days, Dorothy even longer. Maybe he's snowed under with work. I expect Dorothy's stayed up at their cabin. The driveway is quite empty now. A police tow-truck took away the Dodge this morning. I'm sure it's all pretty routine. Perhaps Earl screwed up on the paperwork. It's so easy to make a mistake with these complicated forms. He's always trying to help.

The furnace has been working perfectly for four full days now. The house is lovely and warm. We wanted to invite Connie and Clyde in for coffee this morning but they were at their church. Glenys says we should probably join a local church too. Everyone's so nice.

I've kept quite busy with a small problem with the icemaker in the fridge. It won't stop making ice. It's fine as long as we keep a bucket under the door to collect the cubes as they plop out and we top up the reservoir every four hours or so. It only means getting up once or twice in the night, and at my age I do that anyway.

Tuesday December 20th
I'm really getting the hang of this snow blower now. First I unfreeze the garage door. It only takes a few goes with the hot water straight from the coffee percolator. (We do miss an English kettle here, but no one's ever heard of them in Missoula). Once the door is freed, I've got starting the engine down to a fine art. I rarely have to pull the cord more than a

couple of dozen times. It's so much easier to clear the driveway now that we don't have a vee-hickle on it. And if the snow plough comes, it's no big deal. After all, without a car we can't be blocked in.

Thursday December 22nd
We did our last shop at the Mall today for Christmas. Glenys says she doesn't want to do any more shopping now until well after Christmas. We were hoping to firm up our Christmas arrangements with Gail, but she's not replying to our cell-phone messages. She'll be so busy with such a big party to cater for. Helpful Dean came round and said he'd just check on the furnace. I offered him some of the ice from our fridge but he says he's got plenty.

Friday December 23rd
Connie and Clyde came round today with a Christmas card. Nice to see them again. They brought us a copy of the local newspaper, *The Missoulian*. We were so surprised to see Dorothy's picture on the front page next to that of Earl. There must be some mistake. He's being held in connection with a murder. The paper claims Dorothy disappeared when they went to their cabin in the Blackfoot Valley. Clyde says that the TV reported that police found bloodstains in the snow. I expect it's all a big mistake. Maybe Earl went hunting. They all do that round here. Gun-mad really.
   Later Officer 'Catsick' came round with bad news. They are keeping our truck for a while longer while they examine it carefully. He said they had found stains in it but wouldn't say what of. It looked fine to me when Earl sold it to me. Perhaps I'm right – it's just the paperwork. Poor old Earl. Connie from next door said I was being naïve but I'm not sure what she meant. She didn't need any ice cubes either.
   It snowed quite a lot during the late afternoon, but since we're not doing much tomorrow, Christmas Eve, I told Glenys I'd leave it overnight.

Penthusiasm

Christmas Eve: Saturday December 24th
It was cold overnight and snowed some more so I was busy blowing the snow away today when three police vee-hickles drew up outside and several men got out. They were wearing white overalls and wanted to check our furnace. I said it was working fine at last, but they didn't laugh. Glenys said they were looking very carefully at stains on the floor in our boiler room and on the furnace itself. I expect someone spilled something in there. I told them that Earl's cousin, Helpful Dean as I call him, has been looking after everything. The detectives also seemed pleasant. They asked us not to go anywhere without telling them. I said that apart from visiting Gail and Chuck, we were here to stay. I managed to give one of them a bucket of ice cubes. I told him we were glad to get rid of them.

Christmas Day: Sunday, December 25th
Glenys and I had an extra lie in this morning. We lay in bed and watched the snow falling outside. Then we got up for breakfast. Glenys eats something they call Granola and juice; eggs 'over easy' for me. We're real Americans now, aren't we? We were just getting dressed when the door chimes went. It was Gail. I thought she'd come to fetch us. But she said, 'It's over between Chuck and me.' I think she'd been crying because her eyes were very red. She said that Chuck had another 'girlfriend' who arrived along with his parents. I was surprised. He always seemed so nice. Lucky that we have a big fridge, even if it does keep making ice, ceaselessly. Glenys said she could easily make lunch for the three of us. It didn't matter that we'd not got a turkey. I opened a bottle of Thunderbird. I've discovered that white wine is quite nice with ice cubes in it.

Over lunch Gail explained that things hadn't been good between her and Chuck for a while. She'd hoped things would change but having a baby on the way only made things worse. She said she'd asked her employers to transfer her back to Milton Keynes. They would see what they could do. I thought she was being a little hasty but I didn't say so.

Seven Monmouthshire Writers

After lunch Officer 'Catsick' called. He's so good he even works on Christmas Day. He said that they had found 'traces' in our boiler room which seemed to suggest that the furnace had been used to burn something other than fuel... He wouldn't say what but asked a lot of questions about Dean. I told him Dean had been so very helpful to us. When he left, I pressed him to take some ice cubes as a gift.

I know there have been some surprises here in Missoula but it's been wonderful to have a White Christmas. Everyone's been so nice. Happy Christmas!

Steve Hoselitz

Penthusiasm

ANGELA'S NEW YEAR'S RESOLUTION

In early January I book into a good class hotel - you know the type - they cater for 'reps' on company expenses. I enter the lounge around 7pm, get myself a drink and find a comfortable seat. Before long *they* start to arrive - the reps - these men of a certain ilk, clad in cheap suits, white shirts and drab shoes. Drinks in hand they gather in small groups, talking intensely, each trying to top the other person's sales figures.

They've all noticed me - I'll give them time to have a few more drinks and relax a little.

There is always one guy who will pay more attention to me than the others.

It's my move now. Standing up I nudge the table with my knee just enough to knock my drink over. He's over like a shot: 'Can I help?'

I ask him to grab some napkins from the bar. He's away in a flash and back again with a handful of napkins - he should have been a gundog: 'Let me.'

He sets about mopping up the spilt drink and at the same time he introduces himself: 'I'm Mike.'

'Hello Mike, I'm Angela.'

We shake hands, his strong grip gives me a shiver of pleasure, I put on a show of being impressed which does wonders for his ego. It's my move again.

'Mike, I'm about to eat, I have a table booked in the restaurant. Would you care to join me?'

'Thank you, Angela, I'd be delighted.'

Dinner was excellent. Mike is a good conversationalist, quick-witted, funny and of course he thinks he's onto a good thing.

Dinner over, I reach for my handbag.

Mike responds immediately - they always do.

'Please - allow me.'

Mike produces his Mastercard and signals a waiter who responds by disappearing for a few seconds, then returns to present the bill.

'That's very kind of you, Mike.'
He scrutinises the bill and takes on a pallid look.
'Fine, yes, err um yes, ok.'
He realises that my meal comes to £75 and plus his own he's in for just over one hundred pounds and he can't fiddle it onto his expenses.

On our way out from the restaurant, I link my arm through his, allowing my breast to just brush his upper arm - it always works. Back in the bar, I ask Mike to get some drinks while I visit the 'ladies room'.

I don't go to the 'ladies', instead I go out into the car park where I meet the waiter who took Mike's Mastercard. He not only paid Mike's bill - he cloned the card as well. Together we dash to the hole-in-the-wall cash dispenser around the corner and empty Mike's account. Splitting it 50/50, my boyfriend dashes back to work and I walk calmly to my car and slowly drive away. I retain a mental picture of Mike sounding off to his mates - bragging about his sexual prowess and how some men 'have it' and others haven't. Love him!

Gerald Mason

Penthusiasm

THE BEFRIENDER

What do I want with a friend? I mean I'm all right as I am. It was after my last fall – nothing much, just a few bumps and bruises – and the lady from the council – Sonia, I think her name is, asks me if I'd like to have a new friend. She said she could introduce me to someone who'd come round every week for a cup of tea and a chat and maybe a trip to the shops. Well, I told her straight that's not a proper friend if she's sent by the council and anyway, I prefer my own company rather than listen to some stranger going on about things I've no interest in. Even when our Eric was alive, I'd rather have been on my own and he was good like that – kept to himself – you hardly knew he was there most of the time. Though I do miss him. So anyway, Sonia wouldn't take no for an answer – she's a bossy woman, expect it comes with the job. 'Why don't you try it Edna? You never know, you might enjoy seeing someone new.' Just to shut her up, I agreed but I knew it was going to be a waste of time.

Two weeks later, she arrived on the doorstep - a little wisp of a woman – gust of wind could blow her over, I should think – probably about 60 – same age our Sandra would have been. 'I'm Cynthia from the Befrienders,' she said. 'You must be Edna. Is it all right if I come in?' Well, she soon made herself at home – insisted on making the tea and she'd brought a cake – date and walnut – not to my taste but you have to be polite.

'What sort of things do you enjoy doing, Edna?'

I thought it was a daft question. I mean, at my age, I'm just glad to get through the days and hope my arthritis isn't playing up. The high spots are meals on wheels and *Countdown* – if you call that enjoyment. Anyway, I said something about liking baking and knitting and keeping my little garden tidy – I don't know what she expected but it seemed to cheer her up. After about an hour, she said she'd have to go and then: 'Well, Edna, do you think you'd like me to come over for a little visit every Thursday?' I said, 'Oh, I don't mind if that's what you want.' I didn't want to be rude.

Seven Monmouthshire Writers

So after that, she came round every week, sometimes just for a chat and sometimes we'd go out for a coffee or to do a bit of shopping. It was all right but I couldn't really see the point and she wasn't my friend, whatever she called herself. Then there was one Thursday when we were sitting by the fire having our tea when she starts to tell me a bit about herself – I don't know why. It turns out she's a widow too, lost her husband to cancer two years ago and then she said, 'Oh and I had a son – his name was Stephen – but he was killed in a motor cycle accident when he was nineteen. You never get over it really.' I just sat there, not saying anything, not knowing what to say, and then suddenly I started talking about Sandra. 'I lost my daughter, my Sandra, when she was 22 and just out of university, mown down by a drunken driver when she was walking home. My lovely girl. Eric never got over it but we never talked, we kept it all in.' And the tears just flowed, as I sat there with Cynthia and I thought of all that I'd lost. I realised that she was holding my hand and she was crying too.

I'll make us another cup of tea,' she said.

Maggie Harkness

Penthusiasm

THE POET

Syllables paced across the writer's cell,
the metre marched out on a well worn floor.
Once in magical times things went so well
but cigarettes and booze can help no more.
In anguish thoughts are racked to find that phrase
to fit a line; imperfect now a week.
Outside those people spend their working days
in normal lives which make his own seem bleak.
If he could plumb, or weld, or drive a bus
then he, too, could carefree walk the street,
enjoying the bustle of life's great fuss;
smiling at anyone he chanced to meet.
Instead a vein he opens with his pen
and on the page starts dripping words again.

Hugh Rose

FIGHT

Back - back - back - you shrouded figure
This soul is not for you
Bathed in holy bless-ed light
This heart beats on with all its might

Reap elsewhere in your night black shroud
This soul is not for you
Though soldiers of disease march through my veins
You'll not add me to your deathly gains

Lacking strength, my body weak
You may think me easy prey
But you forget my will of iron
This soul's not ready for the act of dying

So get thee gone, you enemy of life
There's nothing here for you this time
I know one day we'll meet again
Till then begone and leave me to my burning pain

Gerald Mason

Penthusiasm

THE DOG HOUSE

There was no way Freya could miss the post-it note. The bright yellow square was stuck firmly to the green enamel kettle. Tired, after a hard day at work, she read - *Working late - Please take Dennis to the park.*

Damn - the dog. She'd almost forgotten the dog. Maybe she was finally getting used to having it around; getting immune to the smell of damp fur and hair all over her carpet. God forbid.

'Dennis,' she called, 'here boy.' No response. Work colleagues did what she asked but the dog didn't, so she hung up her smart jacket and went in search of the hated creature. She found him in the middle of her Laura Ashley duvet, single-mindedly licking himself with a rhythmical slap of his enormous tongue. Other people inherited step-children who visited once a month, on their best behaviours, she'd got lumbered with a horrible, hairy step-dog, who lived with them 24 hours a day, seven days a week. She grabbed the dog by the collar and hauled him off the bed.

'Bad dog - you're not allowed on the bed.'

The hair-fringed eyes viewed her with contempt, then, with a sigh, he turned his back on her, strolled down the corridor and dropped down beside the front door clearly expecting a walk. Lacking the energy to argue, Freya swapped heels for trainers and grabbed her mother's cast-off old anorak from the hook in the hall. She checked the pockets for dog biscuits and poo bags, attached a lead to the dog's collar and let them both out of the front door.

Dennis set the pace. At the full extent of the lead, he headed down the road as fast as he could tow her along. Once safely inside the park railings, she let him loose and sank onto the nearest bench to catch her breath and thought about the dog.

Before he'd moved them into her flat, Kevin had described Dennis's pedigree as part setter, part collie and part retriever. As far as she was concerned, he'd inherited the worst characteristics of all three breeds. She watched as he raced round and round the park, barking at everything and nothing. After attempting to round up the pigeons, he brought her first a flat football and then an empty burger box. On his final pass, Freya grabbed his collar and as she snapped the lead back on, Dennis delivered a pink mobile phone and grinned at her in expectation of a reward for all his hard work. Freya had a quick look for a possible owner but there was no one around, so she slipped the slimy phone into her pocket. She fed biscuits into the drooling mouth and followed the panting dog home.

Once back indoors, Freya wiped the worst of the mud off his shaggy black coat, poured food into the dog bowl and trapped him in the kitchen. She was too tired to think about feeding herself, so she just poured a glass of wine and settled herself on the sofa with a packet of wet wipes and the phone. It was sticky, but undamaged. Dennis was 'soft-mouthed' and Kevin liked to demonstrate it by making him carry eggs from the fridge. She'd noticed how careful Dennis was with her slippers and wished Kevin was half as careful with her stuff and it wouldn't hurt him to hang up the towels, make the bed or even put the rubbish out once in a while.

Freya remembered how bereft she'd felt when she'd thought she'd lost her mobile. All her contacts gone and no back-up address book. Thank goodness she'd found it eventually, down the back of the sofa...Kevin had just laughed. So, thinking of how the owner was probably feeling, Freya scrolled through the list of names and selected the emergency contact number. Wasn't that Kevin's number, she wondered but why would Kevin's number be on what was clearly another woman's phone. It wouldn't be, would it? Just to put her mind at rest and make arrangements to return the phone to its rightful owner, she dialled the number. Recognising Kevin's voice, she ended the call without saying anything. Her mind whirled with all his excuses - working late, meals out with the boss, drinks with the lads. The pink phone rang almost immediately and vibrated in her hand. She heard Kevin's anxious voice asking:

'Sam, are you all right? Where are you? I've been waiting

Penthusiasm

for ages. I told Freya I was working late.....Sam, are you there?'

Again she ended the call without saying anything – but went straight to the bedroom and stuffed all his belongings into black plastic sacks which she piled up beside the front door and put the dog's stuff on top.

All these weeks he'd been cheating on her, laughing at her, treating her flat like a hotel and her like a kennel maid. She'd naïvely presumed that Sam was one of the lads but he'd been seeing another woman and enough was enough.

It was late by the time Kevin got home, full of apologies and excuses. She heard him out and then quietly handed him the phone. Way beyond angry, she told him, quite calmly, to remove himself, his belongings and his dog - from her, from her home and from her life.

In the weeks that followed, Freya was surprised to find that it wasn't Kevin she missed, but Dennis. True, the house was cleaner and sweeter smelling but she watched enviously as other dog owners played with their pets. She didn't like coming home to an empty flat and missed the excuse to go for a walk every day regardless of the weather. So she began visiting the local Dog's Trust. Not quite sure what sort of dog she wanted she looked in every kennel. She gradually got used to the smell and the noise and got to know some of the dogs but couldn't make up her mind. Then finally, one Saturday morning she saw exactly the dog for her. She found the manager and led him to the pen at the end of the row.

'That's the one I want. Can I have him?'

'Good choice,' said the manager. 'Only came in yesterday. He's a bit big and hairy but he's good natured. The bloke who brought him in said his new girlfriend won't let it in the house. Bit of a mongrel, of course; part setter, part collie, part retriever and answers to 'Dennis' – if he's in the mood.'

Anna Hitch

Seven Monmouthshire Writers

THE BEAT OF THE CITY

March fast and strong to the city beat
Breathe in its sting, fill your lungs with its heat
Feel the throb of the traffic like the blood in your veins
Hear the wail of the sirens and the scream of the planes
Mind your feet - that's a man in rags on the ground
Hold tight to your mobile, be soothed by its sound
But don't look at people, hold your eyes in a glaze
Keep moving, no smiling, just dwell in your haze
Stay strong and separate, no part of this horde
The city demands it, not a place to be lured
Watch out for that cyclist he's aiming to kill
But don't swear, don't shout, keep emotion quite still
Look up at the sky, there's the might of the Shard
There are flats for five million but for you life is hard
Just look at those shops – have the good life they say
But they don't speak to you on your minimum pay
Go down underground and follow the tide
Smell the must and decay, but keep up your stride
Get on the train and fight hard for that seat
Jam in the earplugs; keep your eyes on your feet
So lucky to be here the best city of all
Shame you're too tired and too poor for its thrall

Maggie Harkness

Penthusiasm

EMILY DAVISON

Now, just a fading flicker
way distant on my screen,
flung down and trampled underfoot,
and now – who knows your name?

Wild iron hooves come thundering
the race crowd hoarse with hollering,
heart pounding, thudding, bursting,
pure passion's strength propelling
your frail frame's 'giant leap',
for womankind.

Sorry lovey, what d'you say?
Which way'll I vote?
What, me?
Nah ! Shan't bother – not this time,
Off home to get the tea.

OK – So. . . Few now know your name
You gave your life for us, just the same.
You did it.
We got it:

A voice.
The choice.

Cheers, Em!

Louise Longworth

THE COLOUR GREEN AND THE ARNOLFINI PORTRAIT

'Sir, I have exhausted the possibilities and no-one in the whole of Flanders has that much malachite,' Jean Malouet told his master, Jan van Eyck. 'May I respectfully suggest that you paint the dress in a lovely shade of blue. I can obtain as much lapis lazuli as you need.'

'Don't you think I have already suggested that,' the somewhat irascible painter told his pupil. 'You know what these Eyeties are like. He's made his money, bought the dress and now he wants it recorded. I told him that green would cost more. I told him that it might fade over time but he seems to have money to burn and her family's not skint, either.

'I've tried to get the colour right by mixing Verdigris with some ochres; I've experimented with our supplies of green earth, but that shade of green's a real bugger to match. It's got to be malachite. Have you contacted the studio of that Bosch fellow over in the west?'

'Sir, I have combed the whole of Flanders and no one has enough. Ground or unground, it is just not around.'

'Well, I have accepted the commission and spent some of the down payment so there's no going back now. You will have to travel further afield and get every ounce you can. You'll never buy it all from one place but shop around and buy whatever you can find wherever you can. The Germanic lands may yield some, too. I need to finish this commission by the spring, so you best travel soon.'

'Sir,' said Malouet, touching his forelock, bowing and retiring.

Van Eyck turned back to the canvas. His sitter, Arnolfini, and the woman with the green dress were due to arrive shortly. He was sorry now that he had made them quite so prominent in the picture: he could have made them smaller and then he wouldn't have needed quite so much malachite, but there was no retreating now. They had inspected his

Penthusiasm

sketches and the outline on canvas and it had all been agreed. Why, Arnolfini had even drawn up a contract. Apparently that was the way they did things in Lucca. *Hope it doesn't catch on round here,* Van Eyck thought. He was not expecting such an exacting client. Exacting but in some ways diffident. Why, you only had to look at the way he was holding her hand. And with **his** left hand, for god's sake! OK, so it helped the composition, but who on earth offered their left hand. They'd be talking about that for years to come! That and the green dress.

Steve Hoselitz

Seven Monmouthshire Writers

SNOOKERED

Fergal O'Toolan has been my best friend for as long as I can remember and I hate him. It seems like he always comes out on top in every confrontation we've ever had since we were children; when he could run faster, jump higher, spit further and in fact do everything better than myself. During our teenage years at the local dances, he would cavort with all the girls, leaving me sat against the wall like a pillock trying to look as if I didn't care.

'Ah, Declan,' he'd say in that maddeningly condescending manner. 'You have other qualities. It's just that, so far, they have not revealed themselves.'

We grew up in Dublin where he did better at school and at university and while he went off to earn a fortune as a market broker in London, I went to jail.

I'd got myself involved with a phoney time-share scam that was stupid, ill-conceived and bound to get me into hot water. It did. Six months' worth of choky time among people who taught me about gambling, confidence tricks and generally how to live without working at it. They had me convinced that they were masters of their craft, although, had I thought it through, if they were then I would not have met them in prison.

Ah, well! Over the years I've tried many and various schemes to best Fergal. All have failed. All have cost me money. This time, however, I had the foolproof plan. Fergal fancied himself as the greatest snooker player of all time, and he *was* good. If he had given himself some freedom from his wheeling and dealing, he could undoubtedly have got onto the professional circuit. Not that he needed the money, for he was as rich as Croesus, living in big house luxury down in Cork.

I had him. At last I had him. I'd found Jimmy Byrne, a seventeen-year-old snooker genius who could put snooker breaks together like a jeweller assembling a Swiss watch. At the table he was a joy to observe: an artist in this complex skill of body balance, hand and eye coordination and the

Penthusiasm

ability to focus mentally for long periods in a fixed, concentrated state.

The best thing about him, though, was that he looked such a prat: black hair parted down the middle, ears that stuck out like bat wing doors, large front teeth in an idiot smile and the largest, widest, clear-blue, I'm-a-good-boy-I-am eyes you could ever wish to inflict on an unsuspecting, overbearing friend. I knew. I just knew that if I got them together that Fergal's ego would not allow him to believe this innocent, freaky schoolboy could ever beat him at snooker.

There was the possibility of lots of money to be won in wagers – a thousand a frame, I shouldn't wonder. Of course, I'd have to coach Jimmy in hustling. Start off mediocre then turn on the juice when we had him hooked. Ha! I could see the look on Fergal's face as he handed me great rolls of cash. I wallowed in this delicious fantasy for a while, then set the whole plan up.

'Hello, you must be Jimmy's sister. Is your mother in?' I said to the obviously middle-aged woman who had opened the door.

'Ach! You've more flannel than a cricket team's trousers.' She grabbed my hand and pumped it up and down. 'You must be Father Declan,' she peered into my puzzled face.

'Ah no, Mammy.' Jimmy appeared from behind her. 'Mr Adair isn't a priest. He's an agent for the church. He has arranged for me to play in an exhibition charity match at a convent school in Cork.'

'That's right, Mrs Byrne.' I looked at Jimmy in new-found respect; for a cover story had not even occurred to me. 'It's the convent of Saint Francis Xavier and sure all the money raised is going to the little ones in Africa.'

'Hmm...' She tapped her foot on the door step clearly unconvinced. You could tell that she saw something in me that didn't say church, convent or charity.

'You just look after my son.' She had only recently taken her red hair out of rollers, and the long unruly ringlets writhed, serpent-like, giving her such a look of the Medusa that I was reluctant to meet her eyes. She poked me in the chest. 'I don't want him getting any trouble with those convent girls.'

'Ah, don't you be worrying yourself on that score, ma'am. He won't have time for any of that. Sure, he'll have his stick in his hand the whole...his cue, that is. Did they bring the car?' I asked Jimmy, quickly changing the subject.

'Yes. The Molloy boys drove it up this morning, and then went back to town on their push-bikes. They said there's something wrong with one of the back doors, and they also said to tell you,' he gave a big toothed, idiot grin, 'that their father promised if he doesn't get the car back in good order – you are dead.'

We walked around to the side of the house to look at the car. Connol Molloy owed me a favour. I won't go into details but I had once given him an alibi which, although unbelieved by the garda, could not be disproved and thereby saved him from an embarrassing court appearance. The vehicle he'd chosen for us from his car lot wasn't bad. I know nothing about cars at all so I haven't the clue as to its make, but it was black and shiny and looked ok. I'd asked him for an automatic as I thought that would make driving easier. I knew the rudiments of operating a car, as long ago, I'd taken a few lessons at Gimpy George's driving school. However, after a few accidents, which were not my fault, he'd grabbed me by the throat, shaken his walking stick in my face and shouted: 'Declan Adair, if you ever come near one of my cars again, I will shove this stick up your derrière and run you around the town like a lollypop.'

'I don't suppose you can drive?' I looked hopefully at Jimmy.

'No, he can't.' Mrs. Byrne's bony finger poked me again. 'I told you I don't want him getting into any trouble.'

'Well, what's the problem with this door then?' I asked, as I moved out of range of her venomous digit.

'It won't shut,' said Jimmy. 'Bobby Molloy had to sit in the back holding it closed, all the way up here.'

'Right, let's see if there's any string about to tie it with.' I

Penthusiasm

walked to the rear and opened the boot, feeling secretly pleased that I'd found the release catch by accident. There was no string but a tow-rope – bright red and about an inch thick. 'This will do.'

We wound down both rear windows, threaded the rope through the interior of the car and tied it in a huge bow on top of the roof.

'It looks like a birthday present.' Jimmy was delighted. 'Do you think that it will burst open and a stripper will jump out?'

'Enough of that filth, young man!' His mother cuffed his ear. 'You're not away from the house even and already you've become depraved.'

'Come on, Jim. Jump in and let's get going.' The car started first go, thank God, and when I stamped on the throttle, it shot off, bouncing and jerking onto the road. As we swerved from side to side down the hill, I glanced back in the rear-view mirror where I could see Mrs Byrne with the red snakes dancing on her head. *Oh Jeez, Declan!* I thought. *You'll turn to stone now for sure.*

The country roads coming down from the Dublin Mountains are lined with stone walls. These acted like driving guides as I careered from one to the other a bit like a toboggan going down the Cresta Run. By the time we'd made the flatter lands near Wicklow, I'd more or less got the hang of the steering, throttle and brake.

'I dread to think what the sides of this car must look like.' Jimmy was aghast at my driving.' Connol Molloy's going to nail you to a wall, so he is.'

'No, he won't,' I said with a confidence I didn't feel. Connol and I go way back. Anyhow,' the idea had just come to me, 'I'll tell him that you were driving.'

'You wouldn't. Oh, you swine, you would.' Jimmy became distraught. 'Stop the car. I'm backing out of it, so I am. I'm serious, Declan, I want to go home.'

'For God's sake, Jimmy, calm down. Sure I was only having the laugh with you, you eejit. Of course I won't blame you for the damage. I'll sort it out with Connol. You'll see, he'll be sweet.'

Jimmy settled down and was quiet for a while although he did keep looking at me from the corner of his eye to try and weigh up whether I would really sell him out. We drove off into the hills on country lanes where our battered vehicle with its bow on the roof would not draw attention from a passing patrol car.

'It's getting powerful cold with those rear windows open, Declan. If you'd used string instead of rope, then we would have been able to wind them practically right up.'

'Very good, Einstein. But we didn't have any string.'

'We'd have had some in the house if you'd bothered to ask.' He gave one of his manic grins. 'In the cupboard under the stairs, me mammy has a box with a label on it saying 'Pieces of string too short to keep'. That's a joke.' He was irritated by my lack of response.

'Knowing your Mammy, I thought it was probably true.'

'Well, it is, but it's still a joke for all that.'

More and more, Jimmy complained about the cold until I eventually pulled a flask of poteen from my pocket.

'Here, take a nip of this but don't gulp it for it's a potent brew.'

Jimmy put the flask to his lips and almost immediately a look of saintly serenity spread across his face. To this day I have never seen that flask again.

'Don't they know it's Christmas time?'

'Dear God,' I thought. 'He's away with the fairies.'

Fergal had a magnificent house situated on the cliff tops looking out over the Irish Sea. I pulled in through the wrought-iron gates, rolled down the sloping gravelled driveway and stopped in front of the flower garden.

'We're here, Jimmy,' I said, but getting no response went round and opened the passenger door. He sort of poured out onto the gravel. I picked him up but I knew it was all going to be a disaster when, as I propped him against the car, he sniggered and said, 'Tell me again, Declan, how many points is it for the pink?'

'Is it yourself?' Fergal came out of the house toward us. He looked distinguished, suave and elegant and in fact all of

Penthusiasm

those things that I would like to be myself. I turned to meet him and he embraced me in a warm bear hug.

'Ah, Declan old friend, it's good to see you, so it is. Now, where is your snooker maestro?'

We both stared in disbelief as Jimmy, wearing his most idiot of idiot's smiles, slowly slid down the side of the car and sat on the driveway.

'Haaaa! Haa! Ha!' Fergal bent forward clutching at his midriff. 'Ha! Ha! Oh, Declan Adair and aren't you the greatest eejit was ever put on earth? You're always good for some fine craic but you've excelled yourself this time.' He looked at Jimmy and convulsed again. 'Oh dear, oh dear. I knew that you would be trying to fit me up with a ringer, but where in the name of the almighty did you find this unfortunate boy? And would you look at the car?' The tears ran down his face as his body shook with laughter.

'Well,' I said, shuffling my feet in embarrassment. 'He's in no fit state to play, so I'll have to take him back home.'

'Ah, no you don't,' Fergal held up his hand. 'You promised me some sport tonight and I mean to have it. You will have to play in his place.'

'Say what? I'm not going to play you for money. Do I look like a looney?'

'Declan, mate. Sure, I love you like a brother, but yes,' he laughed and gestured at Jimmy, 'you do look just a leetle teeny bit like the biggest loon I've ever met.'

Suddenly he stopped laughing and pushed his face close to mine. There was a sinister glint in his eyes which had me quite scared for the moment.

'You *will* play snooker against me tonight, and will I tell you why? Because I know all of the bookies in this hemisphere and even own a few of them. If word was ever to get around that you had welched on a deal, then you would have to go to China to get a bet down.'

I felt sick, right in the pit of my stomach. I knew he wasn't joking. He *would* do it. Dear God, as a professional gambler, if Fergal put the mark of Cain on me, then the largest part of my livelihood would disappear. I tried to think positively about the situation. I am a good player. It was not beyond the realms of possibility that I could win. I was lying to myself. I'm an all right player and not in Fergal's league at all.

'Ok, I'll play, but you'll have to spot me a few points, so.'

'I will not. We'll play on an even footing.' He glanced at Jimmy and laughed. 'You never know, the quare fella here might sober up before the night is through and save your bacon.'

The snooker room was a dream to behold. The table itself was an antique with massive, beautifully turned legs and highly polished rails. The cloth was immaculate. So vibrantly green it seemed almost like a living entity. Even the walls were a revelation for, on all sides, stretched taut from floor to ceiling was William Morris tapestry, its luxuriant fabric just there to deaden the click of the balls from the rest of the house. It was a venue far too grand for someone of my modest talents.

The snooker went pretty much as I had expected. Long bouts of safety play from us both, then I would make a mistake and Fergal would clear up to win the frame. I was getting thrashed and losing a fortune, when Jimmy, who until then had been comatose in an armchair, stood up and announced: 'I have to go outside.' He staggered off through the doorway.

Fergal and I looked at each other in alarm and followed. Jimmy made it out of the house and lurched to the rear of the car where, being overcome by an attack of nausea, he doubled over, planting his hands firmly on the boot. The car, not having had the handbrake applied, started to roll forward. Jimmy, thinking to stop it, grabbed hold of the bumper, but going down the slope, it had picked up speed and pulled him off his feet. Still hanging on, he was dragged across the ornamental flower beds as the run-away vehicle crashed through the boundary fence on its way to the cliff tops.

'Let go, Jimmy,' Fergal and I screamed in unison, but to no avail.

I ran and dived, catching hold of his legs in a tackle that would have brought the crowd at Lansdowne Road roaring to

Penthusiasm

its feet. I held on tightly to him as the car went out into the air above the cliff, and then vanished from sight. I waited in disbelief, holding my breath for what seemed like forever, until there was the crash of Connol Molloy's car hitting the rocks in the sea far below.

After that, Fergal became most unsociable. He rang for a cab to take us back to Dublin, all the while making nasty references to my legs and my future need for the services of an orthopaedic surgeon.

The journey home was a nightmare with Jimmy having to make many sick stops. When we finally arrived at his house, I assisted him to the door and rang the bell. It wasn't until Mrs Byrne stood there looking at us that I realised just what a state Jimmy was in. Blood from a cut on his forehead had congealed where it had run down his face. Having been dragged through Fergal's garden and fence, his clothes were torn and muddied. All of this, together with a pale, green face induced by a poteen hangover, made him the most alarming spectacle.

His mother suddenly came out of shock. 'What have you done to my son? You monster.' She reached behind the door to produce a flat headed broom. I had turned ready for flight when she struck me across the shoulders. I ran down the hill with her thrashing away at me with the brush. The cab driver, thinking that I was trying to escape without paying the fare, joined in the chase, stopping every now and then to pick up a rock to hurl at me.

One of these rocks connected with the back of my head, pitching me forward into the smoothing arms of darkness. I was floating in an existence where I had no enemies or rivals, just that feeling of euphoria, experienced when your horse goes two lengths clear in the final furlong.

I woke up in the city infirmary having suffered a severe concussion. It had all been a salutary lesson. I'd lost a lot of cash to Fergal. There was the money to pay for the recovery of the car and recompensing Connol Molloy. Add on Jimmy's fee and cab fare, and it had been altogether an expensive and unsatisfactory venture.

Seven Monmouthshire Writers

All was not lost, however, as while I was in hospital I'd met this young guy who was a genius five card stud player. He could memorise all the cards as they were dealt - never lost a hand. Poker was Fergal's game. All I had to do was organise a game between them and I had him. This time I really had him....

Hugh Rose

Penthusiasm

GETTING ON

Life is hard when you live on a pension
They say you're old and past it, not worth a mention
No fun, no love – just take the medication
But I think I'll say bugger to convention
Write a best seller full of steamy sexual tension
Now that'll be a way to get some attention

Maggie Harkness

THE GLITTER BALL

The glitter ball spins, wildly, to the tune,
reflects a myriad mirror'd choices,
fragmented faces, twirls of skirts.
Swept by silver-slivered blizzards
flashing, swift, over youthful limbs.
Caught in the pulsing rhythm of the plan,
playing out to the music of their time.

Each dancer, in his turn, now slips away,
when, for him, the tempo slows, begins to fade.
The melody, still beguiling, retreats in drifts,
gently melts into a distant tranquil air.
The gaps fill up now, one by one
as eager newcomers - straight pick up the beat –
urgent now, and vibrant with fresh hope.

And the omnipotent sparkling sphere swirls
On and on.

Louise Longworth

Penthusiasm

FAREWELL, KEVIN

I've always found funerals a strain and, if I'm honest, I've mostly managed to avoid them – even when I've been quite close to people. It's not only the obvious reminder that we're all going to peg out one day but they've always struck me as a bit phoney. I mean, one minute the person's alive and they've got the usual faults we all have, plus a few more in some cases I can think of – and then they are dead and suddenly they've become a cross between Mother Theresa and the Archangel Gabriel. It just isn't honest – I always feel the urge to shout out 'But what about the fact he was cheating on his wife for twenty-six years' but you don't do that, do you? You just go along with it and pretend.

But when my Kevin dropped dead six months ago, I realised that unfortunately this was a funeral I couldn't avoid – and, even worse, I'd have to come up with a plan – music, poetry, eulogies – what is it they say now? 'a celebration of his life'. But Kevin didn't like music (apart from Meatloaf and I wasn't having that) and as for poetry....To be honest, there wasn't really that much to celebrate about Kevin or not as far as I was concerned – we hadn't said a word to each other for at least three years. So I'd got my work cut out, I can tell you. Fortunately in the nick of time, I was rescued by Roxanne, Kevin's daughter from his first marriage. She just went on the internet and came up with all sorts of ideas – put the whole thing together in an afternoon - but I drew the line at *Another one bites the dust* – you've got to have some respect. Roxanne and I have had a difficult relationship – she was twelve when me and her father got together and a right stroppy madam she was – and she's still the same aged forty. But you've got to have sympathy – being abandoned by her mother can't have helped her personality.

Anyway on the day of the funeral, everything was going beautifully and I was playing the role of grieving widow to perfection. I even managed a few tears. We'd had a eulogy from Kevin's golfing friend Tony which was mostly about golfing technique and Kevin's capacity for swigging pints in the club house and then Roxanne spoke, quite movingly I thought, about how her dad had taken care of her when her mum walked out and how much she loved him. But then just as the curtains were being drawn around the coffin to the strains of *Return to Sender,* I heard this shout from the back of the chapel. I saw a tall flashy-looking woman, all peroxide and earrings and she yelled out:

'Good riddance to bad rubbish.'

Well, Kevin was no angel but I thought that was a bit much. As the woman strode forwards towards the coffin, Roxanne stepped out in front of her.

'Mum, it's you, isn't it? What are you doing here – why are you shouting like that?'

'Because it was all his fault – he drove me out. I never wanted to leave you but he wouldn't let me see you and then over the years I just gave up.'

At that point the vicar intervened and suggested everyone should now leave quietly and have respect for our dear departed Kevin.

Kevin's ex, whose name is Rita, joined us at the wake and it turns out she's a really nice woman, not the vampire that Kevin described. So it's all turned out well – she and I are now best friends and Roxanne and her mother are re-united after all these years.

So you see – a bit of honesty at a funeral can sometimes be a very good thing.

Maggie Harkness

Penthusiasm

A BIG BIRTHDAY

Pat Williamson watched her great grandchildren chasing an errant chicken down the narrow path between the vegetable plots. She had kept a small patch of grass, but most of the large garden was now used to produce fruit and vegetables and to support livestock – if you could describe hens, geese and rabbits as livestock. Two nanny goats, sisters named Gert and Daisy, provided milk for the whole family with enough left over to make them butter, cheese and yoghurt.

The summer of 2047 had started early and it was still hot and sunny enough to celebrate her birthday with tea in the garden. She had been born shortly after the end of the Second World War, in the early hours of 23rd November 1947. Few of her contemporaries were still alive. Many had died of diseases that were now easily dealt with; others had been lost in the floods of 2020 and some, like her beloved Dennis, had developed one of the few diseases which still defied medical science. It was hard to believe he had been finished almost ten years ago; the health services were very strict on value for money and stringently followed the government guidelines on which diseases could be treated.

Brightly coloured birthday banners and lanterns hung between the apple trees. Tables were laid beneath the UV canopies that sheltered the patio and the last of the summer's wasps buzzed hopefully around the net-covered plates.

'Come on, kids, time for tea.' Her grandson's voice made the goats turn their heads and jolted Pat from her daydream. 'You OK, Gran?' he asked.

'Yes, thank you, Kai, I was just thinking about your grandfather. He would have enjoyed today. He was a great lover of birthdays.'

'Yeah, I remember he was a sucker for cake, especially birthday cake. Always joked about the number of candles and keeping the fire service on stand-by. I can't believe he's gone. I'm glad you still have two more years before you get your present from the President.' David went quiet.

'Come on, kids. Time for tea.' Pat felt her daughter's hand

gently squeeze her shoulder. 'Will you cut the cake and then we can eat. I'm sure everyone's hungry and it'll soon be time to feed the animals and sort the wood ready for the burner. Kai's kids already pumped the water for tonight, so that's one less chore. They still find it fun though I'm sure they'll soon get fed up with it, like the rest of us.'

Three children in brightly coloured sun suits and wide brimmed hats ran up to join their elders at the table. Pat ceremoniously cut the cake and they all began to eat. Pat had been preparing for the party for days. Everything was home-made or home-produced. There was less and less available in the shops and she had gradually learnt how to modify old recipes to use the ingredients that they could produce themselves. She copied all her new recipes onto her blog and made hard copies for each member of the family. Electricity was intermittent in the towns, though here the PV panels and wind turbines produced enough electricity for the household during daylight hours, and storage batteries meant they didn't have to go to bed immediately after sunset.

Once they had finished eating, Pat tapped her knife on her glass to call for order.

'Thank you all for coming today and thank you for all your lovely presents and good wishes. I have had the best birthday ever. But events are moving on in the world. Dennis was right; climate change and global warming are proceeding much faster than the scientists originally predicted. As you all know, the situation in urban areas is getting really difficult, so I think it's time you all came to live here. It's something we've all discussed before, in theory and now it's time for us to put the theory to the test. I have managed to buy an extra field from John next door – he's got no relatives to leave the farm to, so he gave me a good price and he ploughed it for me as well, so it will be ready for planting in the spring. With luck, it shouldn't take any of you very long to pack up and make your way here. I don't think it's safe to wait much longer. Beryl's already started getting rooms ready for you all and we have permission to use a couple of caravans while you make any alterations you need.'

Penthusiasm

A short silence was followed by a whoop from the youngest children. There was a buzz of conversation amongst the adults and then one by one, they strolled up to Pat and quietly agreed to her advice. As dusk fell, the women helped Pat clear the tables and the party moved indoors while everyone made their farewells and set tentative dates for their return.

Once they were alone again, with a pot of tea between them, Beryl cupped her hands around one of the last few china mugs.

'You know they all think you've got two more years, don't you?'

'Yes I know, I always was vain about not looking my age. Now, as your Dad would have said, my vanity's come back to bite me on the bottom.' Pat plucked the thick white envelope from behind the clock and opened it and read:

Congratulations on your 100th birthday.
President Bartholomew would like to thank you for your loyal service throughout your long life.

You have four weeks in which to complete your life's journey. The enclosed will conclude your final journey in ten peaceful minutes after which decomposition will commence. The entire process will take approximately four hours, after which your family may dispose of your remains in any way they wish. Failure to comply with government policy will be dealt with.

Pat pushed the two small tablets out of their blister pack. 'I feel better now I know the family are all organised. You're in charge now, Beryl. So, if it's all right by you, it's been such a wonderful day, I don't think I'll wait those final three weeks. Pour me a glass of that nice port and I'll get on with it now.'

Anna Hitch

MEMORIES

No mortal soul can invade, plunder or embellish memories of sheer bliss. Sweet stolen kisses in romantic places. Tracing the outline of lips and faces. A treasured time. Sights, sounds and smells bringing forth a memory.

Nobody can comfort, destroy, or sooth the memories of sorrow or horror gone before. A traumatic moment jumping into the fore provoked by a photograph, a tune, a date, or an aroma. A shivering terrifying moment.

They are there and always will be. They are our very own.

Boredom provokes numerous forgotten slots from the past. Plunging to the depths or flying to the sky. Hidden gems lurk, secrets never shared, pushed away leper-like by choice, waiting to pounce when a memory awakens.

We can choose to share them or keep them locked away. We can manipulate without criticism if we desire. We can analyse, reminisce, or reflect on them. In silent peaceful moments they can be a comfort. A reminder of our very own unique past.

The heart, racked with pain, can leap forward, triggered by a blink of an eye. And in another moment can spring into happiness accompanied by tears of pure joy.

So let's treasure our memories, and relish in the knowledge that they are personal, to be plucked from within whenever we choose. And nobody, nobody can take them away from us.

Margaret Payne

Penthusiasm

ONE MORE

'One more, just one,' the glutton cried,
'And then I'll stop,' (he knew he lied).
'Eat me, eat me,' the nougat suggested,
'I'm firm and chewy and easily digested.'

'No, choose me,' he heard one scream,
'I'm here in the corner, the peppermint crème;
I'm neat, subdued, a plain chocolate skin
You'll want me again if you bite right in.'

'What about me?' cried the walnut whirl,
'I'm pretty and twisted and quite a girl.
Milky with fondant, a nut on the top
Eat one, eat two, you'll never stop.'

'Hang on a moment,' said Turkish delight,
'I'm sweet, I'm scented, my colour is bright
Those British choices might be OK
But they will all make your teeth decay.'

'You don't want soft,' said the almond crunch
'I think you like hard ones, it's just a hunch.
I'm crispy and crackly, my outside is rough
Bite me and chew me 'til you've had enough.'

'Don't listen to them, and all that kerfuffle
Simple is best – I'm just called a truffle
With me you'll find I can be quite boozy...
Soft and squeezy for the very choosy.'

'I *think* you like fruity,' said raspberry square.
'I'm easy to find with a taste so rare
Some others are sickly, some are too sweet
With me you get nature, ready to eat.'

Seven Monmouthshire Writers

'And what about us,' said classical twins
We're the chocolate version of original sins.'
'I'm soft and chewy,' said the one called toffee
'And I'm more grown up,' said sister coffee.

'I'm eating you all you don't need to worry,'
the glutton confessed. Now, without feeling sorry
his remaining task was to answer this question...
Which *small* one to leave for my wife's digestion.

Steve Hoselitz

Penthusiasm

'WORD' DISCOVERS 'MUSIC'

A love poem

Hi! I'm your new lyric – but words fail me – I'm lovesick.
The moment I heard you, I knew.
You're so elegantly composed - what if I proposed?
I know now - no other will do.

I so love your highs, I so love your lows,
I'm all of a quaver, you see.
I can but semi-breve, when I dare to believe
that you might just, one day, love my prose!

Yes, I put in a pun, 'cos we words like our fun.
I hope you do too - could it be?
How would love ever bloom, were life all doom and gloom?
Could word-playing win you, for me?

But, I soar with your woodwind, I flirt with your fiddles,
My assonance swoons to sway free.
Your drum rolls - so stirring, get my syllables whirling,
Alliteration twists-tongues, to tease me.

Now that I'm written, I'm totally smitten.
My motive – to share your notation.
The love bug has bitten, I'm as weak as a kitten
Pure bliss - your tone - poem variation.

I'm so limp in your presence I can scarce form a sentence,
Although I have drunk not one drop!
My question mark's there for you, I would always be there for you.
Rejection would mean - my full stop.

Seven Monmouthshire Writers

We would make a great couplet; I've so much to say yet.
When I hear your refrain, my heart swells.
Your melody lifts my phrases, enchants and enslaves us.
Could we soon hear those tubular bells?

Oh! My heart's in syncopation - you accept my exhortation!
Now our sweet collaboration will come true!
Your feisty wild staccato fires my passionate vibrato
In crescendo we shall scale the heights, we two.

If I'm waxing lyrical, it's because of this great miracle,
The rhapsody our union will bring.
When, in tune, we're joined together, in 'wholly harmony' for ever,
As one, we'll go - and make the whole world -
SING!

Louise Longworth

Penthusiasm

CHILDREN OF CHOICE

I am intrigued by the latest trend in parenting. I'm sure many of you have come across it. From the grand age of 18 months, parents introduce the child to choices.

It starts almost upon waking, and goes something like this:

'Darling, would you like Weetabix, Cheerios, Sugar Puffs or Coco Pops?'

Instant replies are not always forthcoming from the bleary-eyed infant, so the choice is usually offered again.

Ten minutes later: 'Would you like a drink, darling? Milk, orange juice, apple juice or water?'

Getting dressed time, here we go again:

'Now, would you like to wear the blue tiger jeans and the red tee shirt, the green giraffe trousers with the white tee shirt, or the new blue stripy trousers that Nana bought last week?'

After some negotiation, the little person is now dressed and here comes the next choice of the day:

'Would you like to go to the swings down the road, the big supermarket, or feed the birds in the park? Okay sweetie, now whilst Mummy gets dressed, would you like to watch *Ceebeebies, Thomas the Tank* or the *Three Little Pigs*? Lovely, now where would you like to sit, on the floor, on the big cushion, or on the sofa?'

Twenty minutes later: 'Okay darling, Mummy's ready. Would you like to wear your orange and yellow jacket, your fluffy coloured jumper, or your denim jacket? You can go and choose your shoes now. The white trainers and wellie boots are by the front door and your brown trainers are under the bed.'

Not two years old, not midday and the child has already had to cope with making all of these choices. As an onlooker, I'm shattered just thinking about it!

What's wrong with parents? Can't they make a decision? Are they afraid of the child? Did they feel deprived as kids, not being allowed to make choices? Do they have to fill every speck of air with so many words and so many choices? What's wrong with silence sometimes, with making a grown-up decision and just taking control?

The day progresses. Through several lunch choices, and through afternoon activites and healthy snacks. Choices of food, choices of games, choices of pyjamas and finally choices of a bedtime story.

No wonder these children are exhausted by the end of the day. Because along with choices is the very complex task of making a decision. And we all know well as adults, through a lifetime we have to make heaps of them. Not always getting our preferred choice. This will be difficult for the children of the 2000s.

It would be very interesting to try the following approach one day:

'Here we are, darling, Weetabix and a slice of honey toast. Mummy will get you a drink of orange juice in a minute. Today we are going to the supermarket to buy some food for lunch, so put on your blue trousers and green top, and I'll fetch your shoes. There we are, Mummy has put *Teletubbies* on for you whilst I get ready.'

I'm not saying that we should never give our children choices, but surely as we have done with so many things today, have we gone too far? The 'choice kids' may be in for a real surprise when they start nursery class. Will they buck at being told what to do? Or on the other hand, they may find it quite refreshing to be told what to do for a change. Pressure off. It's a gamble.

On reflection of my own children's upbringing in the 70's, I certainly deprived them of choices so young. There was so much to do in the course of a day that it was far easier to take control. Spoon feeding got that chore out of the way much faster. Evening meals had to be on the table on time for the husband, so once again, most daily chores were decided by me. Did I make a mistake? Did I deny them an opportunity to expand their intelligence? Did I deprive them of making decisions? Well, I think not. They were too busy finger painting, chasing the cat and sticking and gluing at the table, choosing colours of paint and biscuits. Yes, they chose ice-

Penthusiasm

cream colours (wow, yes, they ate ice-cream that young, and rice pudding and cakes), they chose sweets (yes, chocolate and chewy things), they chose story time books etc etc but the normal mundane routines of life were definitely made by me.

Moving swiftly on to my childhood in the 50's, it was apparently even easier. No choice of coat, I had one. No choice of school shoes, I had one pair. No choice of evening meal, only one was cooked, and no choice of TV programme, we didn't have one! Yippee.....

Margaret Payne

Seven Monmouthshire Writers

GAILY TO THE CEILIDH

Sure - t'was a wondrous ceilidh,
we danced from dusk to dawn,
when Patrick wed his Mary
- and Bridget kissed Shivaun!

The priest's face was like thunder,
boding ill for both the lasses,
but it was all smoothed out
when it was pointed out
Bridg had come without her glasses!

The fiddlers played as if on fire,
we twirled, we dipped, we sang.
two hundred voices, young and old.
and yes – those rafters rang.

Flanagan's shenanagans
had everyone in fits,
'til he tried to leap like Nureyev,
and the eejit did the splits!

When the ambulance had finally gone
we carried on all night,
it turned out it was just the shock,
- the Guinness put it right!

It flowed, fast as the Liffey,
Nose-nudging creamy froth
meeting teasing fine aromas
from Ma Murphy's mutton broth.

We staggered out at six am,
full of love and stew and craic,
Shivaun and Bridg were missing though,
They were somewhere out the back!

Louise Longworth

Penthusiasm

DIANA

To love, honour and cherish, to forsake all others
This binding oath before God and the queen
The pomp and the ceremony - so loved by the masses
The finest wedding the world's ever seen

They stood for the photos - the applause of the crowds
They impressed the whole world - such a fairy tale wedding
They were honoured and blest - the whole day was hallowed
His words however, were pathetically shallow

This beautiful lady we thought would be queen
Was chosen by Charles as a breeding machine
And having produced sons for the heir to the throne
Charles just ignored her and went back to his crone

The crone lurked in shadows - just out of sight
With complete disregard to Diana's sad plight
Charles and the crone continued their affair
They turned their backs on Diana who fell ill with despair

Such a disingenuous nature - this heir to the throne
Along with his partner, the disingenuous crone
But people still revere them - they've got away with their crime
As for me, I'm referred to as that Leftwing Philistine.

Gerald Mason

Seven Monmouthshire Writers

WOULD LIKE TO MEET

The appropriately named botany master Mr Kenneth Plant had been married to the timid Latin Mistress, Ginnie Anderson, for twelve years before the split. Improbably tall and thin, he had towered over her diminutive figure by a good fourteen inches. His heavy thatch of thick brown hair contrasted starkly with her wispy blonde bob. He drove an elderly Austin 7 which he would occasionally pack with favoured students for trips to nearby Cambridge. Rumour has it that once, when being instructed to go 'straight across' the next roundabout, he had indeed driven straight across the roundabout; mounting the grassy hillock with a teeth-loosening jar and bouncing off again the other side with a jolt that had threatened the ageing springs.

With much soul searching he had reached a difficult decision. For the sake of his three small daughters, he must put his wife's betrayal behind him and find himself a new wife – a mother for his girls. Oblivious to the faint odour of formaldehyde, he threaded his long arms into the sleeves of his worn tweed jacket, straightened his tie and set off for the town hall. He had seen the flyer pinned to the notice board in the sixth form common room; not that the boys were allowed into town after 6pm. 'Speed Dating' the latest craze from America; it was advertised as the quickest way to make new friends.

His arm was grabbed almost before he'd got through the door.

'Hi, I'm Katriona, your cupid for the evening! Write your name on this label, stick it on your jacket and then MINGLE. There's Caribbean fruit punch over there. First glass is on the house. When you hear the bell, sit at one of the tables, with your back to the wall.'

He'd barely had time to taste the sickly, rum-flavoured concoction from the plastic glass thrust into his hand by a blousy woman, well past her best, when the bell rang. He folded his long frame into a metal chair and gazed at the woman sitting opposite him.

Penthusiasm

'Hi,' she said, thrusting an unfettered bosom at him. 'I'm Candice; well, you can see that from my label.'

He dragged his eyes from the quivering flesh to the label attached to her straining t-shirt. Childish letters in purple marker, complete with a heart over the i.

'So what do you do, Ken?' she asked and then without waiting for him to reply, continued, 'I am a nail technician, ever so skilful it is. I've got my own booth outside Boots in the shopping Mall. I applied for a pitch outside Debenhams, but they said they'd got their own nail bar so I had to move down fifty yards or so. Do you know I can French manicure, paint any design of your choice or inset diamante – whatever turns you on. What turns you on, Ken? I can call you Ken, can't I?'

Unsure how to reply, he was relieved to hear the bell ring. Katriona clapped her hands and shouted:

'Right...now....all you men move to the table to your left and meet your next partner.'

After some initial confusion about which way was left, Mr Plant found himself seated opposite another available female. He looked at her carefully to check that she really was alive. Utterly motionless, she barely seemed to breathe, staring unblinking at a spot of green acrylic paint on the corner of the table between them, which he assumed was a legacy of the morning's toddler group.

He waited. Nothing. All around the sound of conversation from the other tables felt like an accusation. He took a deep breath.

'Hello, Jane,' he said, reading the label stuck far away on her right shoulder. Nothing. He tried again. 'Hello, Jane, I'm Kenneth.'

Finally she shifted slightly in her seat and peered up at him through greasy glasses.

'No, you're not,' she said, 'You're Mr Plant. You taught me human biology.'

Once more, with burning cheeks, he was saved by the bell. He moved to the next table along. *Could it get any worse,* he wondered? It could indeed. As he raised his head to check the label on the striped jersey sitting opposite him, his eye was caught by a familiar face, though he couldn't remember whose mother was sitting there waiting for him.

'Hello, Mr Plant.'

Was there no escape?

'Excuse me,' he said, 'got to go,' and pushed his way past the last five tables and out through the fire escape. Waiting for his heart rate to return to normal, he leaned against the dust bins and wished he still smoked.

'You look like you could do with one of these,' said a young blonde woman who was sitting on an upturned milk crate. He took the proffered cigarette with shaking hands.

'I don't smoke,' he explained.

'Me neither,' she replied as they both concentrated on smoking, inhaling deeply and savouring the taste.

'Well, that's something we've got in common, isn't it? Both non-smokers! Got any kids?'

'Yes, three little girls; you?'

'Yes, I've got three too. Three Two!' she shook her head and laughed nervously. 'Twin boys and a girl; their father waltzed off with a wisp of a woman who left her kids behind. What woman does that?'

'It happens,' he said, 'you'd better believe it. I can't face going back inside again, but I don't need to go home just yet. Have you got time for a drink?'

'Oh yes, please, I'd love a coffee. You lasted longer than me in there, you know. All that MINGLING, by the time the third man had told me I'd taught his kids, I felt fat, old and frumpy. I didn't teach your kids, did I? I work at Layfield Primary.'

'No – I didn't teach you, did I? I work at Townend High and after this evening, I feel like Methuselah.' He tucked his hand under her elbow, led the way round the dust bins and out on to the High Street. 'There's a new independent down there on the right. Let's go and get that coffee and perhaps we can discuss what we could do together before we're old enough to collect our bus passes.'

Anna Hitch

Penthusiasm

RUN FOR YOUR MIND

That hospital was a disappointment to me; I mean, a shrink who doesn't have a couch is like a politician without a smile. All he had was a stupid chair – a synthetic pretence of leather, which under cover of my every move, broke wind, putting the blame on me and, although he must have known, he glared as if I actually had. His hands were covered in black curly hairs which I think I've heard is a sign of insanity. His eyes were plops of grey in white bulges - like the pigeon droppings on my window sill. For a long time we sat in silence, separated by a plastic desk. I swear that I could hear the hairs growing from the backs of his hands.

'Shouldn't we talk?' I said, unable to bear it any longer.

'Aha!' He wrote a note into my file as though I had said something really incriminating. 'What do you want to talk about?' He sounded pissed off.

I didn't think we had anything in common but I tried him on movies. I asked him if he'd ever seen *The Grapes of Wrath* starring a very young Henry Fonda. It wasn't as good as John Steinbeck's book but...

'That's who you remind me of.' He broke his pencil.

'Who? - Henry Fonda?'

'No, Simon Bradshaw.' He gave me one of those teacher's looks, you know what I mean? Like when they think they've caught you doing something disgusting. 'You look the sort who wears a silk cravat and drinks double pink gins at the golf club on Sunday mornings.'

I tried to explain that I was in that place because I'm an alcoholic and my tastes and pockets run more to red biddy than gin, even if it's pink, but he wouldn't have it.

'You're the sort who seduces a chap's wife in the rough while a chap's stuck in a sand bunker without a wedge.'

I said that even women who liked a bit of rough steered clear of smelly winos like me.

He started jumping up and down with both feet together, so I rang for the male nurse. Big Rupert came in and, although I wasn't making a fuss, wrapped his arms around me. Old Rupe is as bent as a docker's hook and can't resist handling the merchandise.

The shrink was weeping now making pigeon droppings run down his face. 'Take that swine out and give him a lobotomy.'

'We can't actually do that any more, Doc.' Rupe gave me a wink and a friendly grope.

'Well, fill him up with junk and put him on tomorrow's roster for electro-therapy.'

Rupe took me down to the dayroom and gave me a handful of pills which I swapped for three cigarettes with an old guy who was a walking catheter.

I broke out of there that night and took it on the toes. I haven't had a drink since because I'm terrified of being caught and I don't think my mind could take the strain of being normal.

Hugh Rose

Penthusiasm

WAKES AWAY

Breathe in that air look out at the sea
For one week a year it's a time to be free
From the grime and the grind and the days of despair
This is the place you can let down your hair
And act daft if you want and wear kiss-me-quick hats
Feel the surf on your toes and flirt with the lads
There's nowhere like Blackpool it makes your heart race
You can ride on the donkeys and dance down the beach
You can walk on the prom, feel the sun on your face

When you gaze out to sea what's there beyond reach
Another life there might be from the factory floor
Away from the smoke and the noise and the chore
Maybe one day there'll be more than this week
To dance and to play and to bathe in the deep

Maggie Harkness

THE SCULPTOR

Fine slivers of shavings. Gauze-thin. Translucent.
Cascade - lightly pattering, to litter cool tiles.
No other sound in the studio, but the sculptor's fast heartbeat,
But life pounds on - in echo, outside on the street.

Sunlight streams down through the cobweb-edged fanlight,
Glinting on chisel as it shapes and refines.
Layer succeeding impassioned veined layer,
Until dusk at last creeps in to replace dawn and day.

The artist works on in the stuttering candlelight,
Until chisel at last fails his fast-tiring hand.
And he slumps, fighting sleep, by the tall mass of marble,
Drifts to dreams of the figure he knows awaits there.

At the first gentle hint of the dawn call of birdsong,
He leaps up - refreshed – in a frenzy to start.
Coaxing – encouraging the emerging revelation.
Until one day he steps back. Knows it's right. Knows it's done.

She returns his gaze. Radiant. Serene in her gratitude
to the one who was blessed with the vision to see
what all others had passed; unsuspecting; unknowing,
Now the long wait is over.
She's found – and she's free.

Louise Longworth

Penthusiasm

TALL TALES

I guessed that something was wrong as soon as she extended her foot towards me. It was never going to fit inside that small glass shoe. Actually, I immediately felt a wave of relief. My partner in *Strictly* at the Palace last night was an angel on the dance floor; not this gorgon sitting in front of me now, nor her sister, equally overbearing, who was standing behind her...

It's been a morning of similar revelations.

Earlier, I'd heard about the small and ruddy faced kitchen maid, who luckily sensed that something was wrong when she went to visit her granny in the house in woods and found an imposter with a hairy face and dog-breath. You just can't rely on Social Services anymore!

And the laundry maid, Snow White (or is that the soap powder she uses, I forget now) is off sick. Apparently she'd guessed something was wrong with that apple as she bit into it. A date rape drug, I expect. That doesn't usually have a pretty ending, does it?

There are jobs to do round the estate but we're getting little sense out of our elderly handyman, Geppetto, who says he was whittling away at a piece of old twig, when suddenly 'it started talking to him'... I don't think so. We're going to have to let him go, I'm afraid.

Mind you, we've been plagued with tall stories for quite a while now. Back in the spring Jack, the son of one of our employees – ex-employees I should say – cut down our prized trumpet vine, babbling on about giants! And the week before, his brother had been reprimanded after shutting all our pigs in their sties, wittering on about straw and sticks.

Then there was the strange incident with the housekeeper's daughter, that girl with the blonde hair, what was her name, who made out she'd been consorting with bears. Bizarrely her mother blamed it on a faulty packet of porridge from the supermarket. Faulty parenting, more like!

Seven Monmouthshire Writers

There's talk of a house made of biscuits... Nice! And some bloke with a pipe playing music to rats. And some of the stories from further afield are pretty grim.

Anyway I can't hang around gossiping with you like this: I've got work to do.

If you want me, I'll be up in the tower with the miller's daughter. We've had a fresh delivery of straw so there's gold to spin.

Steve Hoselitz

Penthusiasm

A NOVICE'S GUIDE TO THE ABERGAVENNY FOOD FESTIVAL

There are several basic guide-lines that, if followed, will enhance the experience of the novice festival goer.

Register with the Official Food Festival web site and you will receive details of the coming festival as soon as they are published. This will hopefully guarantee that you will secure tickets for your chosen events. Don't hesitate or the most interesting events will already be filled with those in the know.

Try to include at least one foodie in your group. They have an in-built ability to identify those celebrities who will provide the best entertainment and they will lead you with their noses (and palettes) around the stalls and exhibits ensuring that no tasting opportunity is missed.

Organise transport to the festival so you do not have to drive. There's plenty of parking but many of the master classes and tastings are accompanied by generous amounts of alcohol. Drinking and driving is not only illegal, it's dangerous. However, it's criminal to attend a masterclass and have to refuse the accompanying wine.

Arrive hungry. There are countless opportunities to try and to buy; local, national and international cuisine, from the common to the obscure. Fast food stalls provide sweet or savoury, familiar or exotic something for everyone. The town's cafés, pubs and restaurants also offer festival-goers anything from a full English (or Welsh) to coffee and cake to a fine dining experience.

Wear comfortable shoes. Abergavenny may be a small town but there are venues all the way from St Michael's Centre to the Castle, from the fish market behind the Priory Centre to the Farmers Market beside the Post Office as well as the market hall, its car parks and the street markets in between.

Allow plenty of time. If you want to attend some ticketed events and still have time to see all the exhibits – book a full

Seven Monmouthshire Writers

weekend pass. If you are content to pick and choose, then one day might be enough for you. Saturdays are busiest - vibrant and exciting. Sundays are slightly quieter – with a more relaxed atmosphere.

When you get home, put your feet up, pour a glass or two of festival wine and while you nibble on festival snacks, read the advertising leaflets and the recipes you've collected and happily contemplate doing it all again next year.

Anna Hitch

Penthusiasm

THAT GHASTLY PURPLE THING

The fractured melody of the front door chimes brought the inevitable grumble from Ethel. She had been enjoying a lively argument with Jenni Murray. Ethel always joined in the debates on *Woman's Hour* by shouting invectives at the radio. 'Bloody silly woman, wouldn't know a good hymn if she fell over one,' she fumed as she shuffled in her slippers into the hall. 'Who is it?' she called out. She received no answer so put on the safety chain and opened the door a crack. A man in a light brown suit stood outside. His shoes were black and dusty which meant that he went straight into Ethel's pigeon hole for useless human beings. With that suit, he ought to be wearing highly polished dark tan Oxfords. 'What do you want,' she said making no attempt to hide her belligerence.

'Good morning, Madam.' She thought she could catch a trace of a foreign accent that she couldn't quite place. Perhaps it was Polish or Ukrainian. No, Newcastle, that was it. Like those two annoying little chaps off the television – Anton something or other.

'What do you want? she asked again.

'I'm a financial advisor. My company has come up with an offer that can enable pensioners to enjoy the value of their homes without having to sell them.'

'I already enjoy my home, thank you very much. Now go away.'

'Really, Madam, if you would allow me to come in, I could explain the plan to you.'

She thought he sounded a bit angry now and she didn't like his eyes. They were a strange colour, neither blue nor grey and not slate either. They had something slimy about them like garden slugs. That was it – slug grey, he had slug grey eyes.

'You are most certainly not coming in,' she said. 'And if you don't go away, I'll call the police.'

She shut the door and locked it. She went over to the hall

window but couldn't see the man. He had gone from the door but wasn't on the path or the pavement.

'Oh my God, he's gone round the back.' She ran through the house to the kitchen. The back door was closed but unlocked; she turned the key and slid home the bolts. She couldn't see him from the kitchen window either. Where had he got to? He couldn't have got in before she locked the door, could he? She would have heard him, wouldn't she? She made a tentative look into the dining room but saw no one in there. Oh no, please not down there. The passageway to the inside garage door had a low ceiling which even under normal circumstances gave it an air of menace. She'd named the garage The Crypt of the Damned because of its damp, dark coldness and the mournful acoustics from its bare brick walls.

She started speaking to herself out loud, gaining comfort from the sound of her own voice. 'He couldn't really have come into the house – why would he? What could he possibly want with me? Although it has to be said, those Eastern Europeans are weird, look at that Count Dracula chap that I saw on television the other night. He came from Transylvania. Mind you, I wouldn't mind having Louis Jordan sucking on my neck. For goodness sake, Ethel Bellamy, get a grip. This is neither the time nor the place to be thinking of such stuff. Anyway you decided that he came from Newcastle. Yes, but there again, they can be a bit odd as well.

'If you're in the garage I warn you I've got a savage dog that I'm going to send in there after you.' She made what she hoped was a savage dog type growl: 'Grrrowl! Good boy, Satan.'

From the corner of her eye she thought she caught a movement behind her and was convinced that someone had run out of the dining room and up the stairs.

She ran into the hall and shouted, 'I know you're up there, I'm calling the police.'

She went into the sitting room, shut the door and leaned against it. She should call the police really but if it were all in

Penthusiasm

her imagination again, it would be yet another nail in the coffin of her independent living. Her daughter was already anxious to have her moved into a retirement home and would seize on such an opportunity. What a pity that young David from over the road was out at work. He was a policeman and would have come to her assistance without having to tell the world about it.

On *Woman's Hour* a caller had just rung in from Chipping Sodbury and was saying in a high pitched voice: 'Blake had it completely wrong about Jerusalem. We are a long way from the Middle East so those feet could not possibly have walked on this green and pleasant land.'

'Metaphorically, dear,' growled Ethel as she switched off the radio. 'Metaphorically.'

She strained to listen for alien noises but could only hear the hollow ticking of the grandfather clock. Tick, tick, tick. Strange how she had never before noticed how remorseless it sounded. Tick, tick, tick: as though it were saying: 'I am time and I've got my eye on you.' She gave a shudder which turned into a chill as she heard a thump on the floor above, then another and then – yes, someone was coming down the stairs, two at a time by the sound of it. She picked up the poker from the fire place and stood behind the door with the weapon raised ready to strike. Her heart began to bang about inside her chest, making such a racket that she could not now hear the clock.

She kept her eye on the door handle; he would open it at any moment. He was there. She could feel his evil presence seeping through the wooden fibres. She could bear it no longer and snatched open the door.

'Oh, Shostakovich, you naughty boy, you scared the life out of me.'

A huge Persian cat, with fur almost the same colour as Ethel's hair, sauntered into the room with an air of practised indifference.

She leaned against the door again, her bosom heaving as she tried to regain her composure and miracle of miracles, David had come home. He was parking his car outside his house. She rushed across the room, opened the window and shouted: 'David, please. I need help.'

He tore over the road to her window. 'What is it, Mrs B? Have you had an accident?'

'No, I think I've got an intruder. A man came to the front door and I sent him away but I think he got in through the back. I think he's upstairs.'

'Ok. Now you calm down. Let me in, I'll soon sort this for you.'

She went into the hall and opened the door.

'Oh, you poor thing,' he said as he hugged her. 'You're shaking. It's all right, there's no need to be frightened any more. I won't let anyone hurt you.'

She could feel his strong arms around her shoulders as she buried her face into his pectoral muscles. *This is the best I've felt all day,* she thought and then: *Come off it, Ethel Bellamy, this is the best you've felt for years.*

'Now then,' he said looking into her face. First I'm going to have a good look around down here. I want you to stay in the hall to make sure that if Chummy is upstairs, then he can't escape without me knowing about it. If you see him, just shout as loud as you can and run to me. Under no circumstances are you to try to stop him.'

There's no danger of that, thought Ethel. *I don't like waiting here on my own. Chummy might run down the stairs and overpower me before I can get away. I must say that Chummy's a funny name to give him. It sounds sort of friendly. He didn't look like a Chummy to me, more like a Vlad the Impaler.* She almost screamed as a hand touched her shoulder.

'It's all right,' said David. 'I've been right through and there's no one down here. Now you go and relax in the sitting room while I check upstairs.'

'No blooming fear,' she said and followed after him. 'I think it was in my room that I heard him.'

David pushed the door open and searched the room; under the bed and behind the curtains. He opened the wardrobe doors and – oh horror! She still had that awful purple outfit.

Penthusiasm

Dear God, I thought I'd got rid of that monstrosity, years ago. Please, please don't let David notice it, he'll wonder what sort of tasteless creature I am.

'There you are,' he said brushing his hand along the dresses. 'Nothing in there either.' To her relief he closed the doors and went out to complete a similar check in the other two bedrooms, the bathroom and even the airing cupboard.

'Ok, Mrs B, that chap didn't come in after all. But I'm glad that I've been able to put your mind at rest.'

'You won't tell Eileen about this, will you?' she begged.

'No, of course not, but I do think that you ought to get a panic alarm. What would happen if, God forbid, you should have an accident like falling down the stairs? I'll drop you in some leaflets tomorrow.'

She watched from the sitting room window as he went back over the road.

'What a lovely, lovely man. I hope his wife appreciates what she's got. Because so many of them don't nowadays. They all think that the grass is greener somewhere else. Talking of colours, I'm going to get rid of that ghastly purple thing before I forget.'

She went up the stairs thinking: 'I'll stuff it in the bottom of a bag and put it out for the bin men. I won't take it to the charity shop. I don't want that snooty Mavis Evans thinking that I ever wore such a thing.'

She opened the wardrobe doors and two hands shot out from within the dresses to grab her by the throat. So sudden was the attack that her larynx had started to collapse before she had chance to make a sound. Her body went into shock and, but for the strength in those hands and arms she would have fallen. She hung there a pathetic dangle off the floor and the last thing she ever saw was a pair of slug grey eyes staring at her from the back of the wardrobe.

Hugh Rose

ALL IN A NIGHT'S WORK!

Another night's work shrivelled and limp. These lumbering shadowy objects have no consideration at all. My beautiful creation wrecked by a poke. Took me an age to find and establish a good bridge and wait for a gentle breeze. Don't they realise spinning takes a lot of effort? My spinnerets are getting old now and running up and down these branches is hard. I always rest in the daytime, but come evening, I set to work again, always wondering how far I will get before my gossamer threads are attacked. Of course, I get good days, when my work gets finished. I can sit in the centre of my creation and wait for a fly snack to arrive. Such is a life of a spider.

Margaret Payne

Penthusiasm

GOODBYE DEAR JAKE

Good-bye dear Jake, we had to let you go
The hardest thing we've ever done because we love you so
We'll miss you in so many ways, the house feels dull and dark
No morning greeting, cheery wags or that excited bark
In human years one hundred was the age you would have been
I really think you should have got a message from the Queen
So skilled at greeting people a nose touch of their hands
Friends who said 'I don't like dogs' would soon be doting fans
You never were a good dog, always up to tricks
Chocs and cheese would disappear and you would lick your lips
For us, you see, you were life and joy and fun
So very sad to know that you have truly gone
But no, I see you now - running, tail high, ears askew, coat glossy in the sun
You were our very special dog and in our memories you will live on.

Maggie Harkness

WORD PLAY

'Word' was happy - tumbling out,
so failed to see the point
when the stranger - 'Punctuation' - waltzed right in, to rule
the joint.
         So declared

I'll babble if I want to! Why should I stop and start?
How dare he make me hyphenate
 - upset my apple-cart!

It seems that he claims different names - just why I fail to see,
Punctuation 'Mark' - Exclamation 'Mark',
Well - my Question 'Mark's - why me?

Why restrict my freedom - stop my gallop in its prime!
sentence me to Paragraphs -
state missed Commas are a crime?

Don't want to pause, or form a clause - the interfering clot,
and this affection for the Colon -
Guys – it's just a double dot!

I want to fascinate, not punctuate -
forget the Forward Slash.
It's stifling my artistry – new-fangled balderdash!

Mind - his Capitals are - rather fine,
and I - quite like it - all in Bold,
although I'd like to underline, that Full Stops leave me cold!

I confess – I may be softening, to the warm hug of the Bracket,
and the Apostrophe has taken hold,
now I've got the knack of it!

Penthusiasm

The relationship is deepening, and the chemistry – Oh Glory!
And we've made a date,
to – collaborate.

But that's another story!

Louise Longworth

THE DAYS OF CHARS

I suppose you would describe Mrs Potter as 'plain' if you were trying to be polite: actually in common parlance, she was downright ugly and, quite wrongly, we were scared of her. She had heavy features and a lantern jaw which seemed to shape her whole face so it looked like a grubby pink bean-bag. She had two dark spots which you simply could not ignore, one on a nostril and the other, sprouting whiskers, on her chin. Her slightly gingery hair was always drawn back and tied in an untidy bun on the back of her head, kept in place by a coarse hairnet. Ena Sharples comes to mind.

Normally I believe you can see someone's personality in their face, but if you tried to read Mrs Potter's, you'd come up with the wrong answer. She looked stern and unkind, cruel even. Which is why we children were scared of her. But in reality, she always tried to be obliging. She went about her tasks with a kindly air even if, with her prominent pout, it might have seemed as if she'd just been tricked into performing yet another unacceptable chore.

On Thursdays - that was her day with us - she would be found at some stage, scrubbing brush in hand, on her knees cleaning the scullery floor, working backwards from the passage towards the kitchen. Her un-feminine hands, red from the hot caustic water, were almost the same colour as the scarlet quarry tiles. She scrubbed the floor first, then mopped it with a rag wrapped over an old sweeping brush head, making it only slightly drier. Cleaning equipment rinsed out in some dubious water. My mother, provider of the sub-standard equipment, saw nothing wrong with any of this. And if she knew Mrs Potter's first name, I never heard it mentioned. It was always Mrs Potter this, Mrs Potter that. 'Mrs Potter's here tomorrow, so tidy your room', I'd be told on Wednesday when I got home from school. Or 'Mrs Potter's just scrubbed that floor so take your shoes off.'

Mrs Potter was with us for years, always wearing a printed cotton wrap-over thingummy to cover her otherwise dull

Penthusiasm

clothes. Summer or winter, rain or shine, she would arrive wearing a thick, heavy coat which she'd take off and hang somewhere in the passage; she appeared to think that her coat was not entitled to be hung in the cloakroom under the stairs where all our family's coats were hanging.

At the end of 'her hours' she'd put the money my mother left, in her purse and go back into the passage for her coat. Then tying a triangle of scarf round her head, she'd chime 'God Bless', and crunch down the path to the pavement.

As you might have gathered, Mother was by no means particularly house-proud, so in one sense, Mrs Potter had it easy. Much easier than a succession of gardeners, over whom she would stand and glower as they did some weeding. For some reason, gardeners were never entitled to be called 'Mr' (not that mother was a snob) so it was 'Fox, don't touch that, it's a bulb', or 'Fox, you have pruned that too hard'.

By contrast I never heard my mother complain to Mrs Potter about the standard of her housework. This was never going to be more than adequate at best, given the tools with which Mrs Potter was expected to work. Typical was our Hoover, which had a dangerously worn flex and a slipping belt so it had about as much suck left in it as a miner's lung, and sounded similar.

What our char must have thought of us, I cannot guess. She bravely put up with my mother's 'economy' equipment and materials including stinking dishcloths, smelling of drains and made of torn squares of old towels. Surely she must have been puzzled by a household which could afford a char but couldn't stretch to decent materials.

We never knew what she thought because Mrs Potter was not a talker. By the time she'd been coming for a few months, my sister and I got over being scared of her and decided she was not really the cruel witch or child-torturer we'd assumed. But long before we could befriend her, she stopped coming. I never did find out why but perhaps she'd found someone who supplied proper cleaning equipment.

From then on things were very different.

We lived not far from one of those labyrinthine mental hospitals which had been built round many major cities in the late 19th and early 20th centuries. Cane Hill supplied my mother with a succession of char ladies, all of whom cheerfully put up with the wheezy vacuum and my mother's penny-pinching approach to household management. None of them ever had first names, either. And each of them brought their own brand of originality to the job of keeping 'Number 97' clean.

Mrs Wraith, small and slight, lasted for all of two months before she finally decided that the pictures on the walls were moving. She was succeeded by Mrs Littlewhite, who had a hunted look about her. She lasted a little less long and just stopped coming. Then there was Mrs Gunter (whom I called Grunter - but not to her face!) She decided on her fourth or fifth visit that the pebble dash on the outside of the house needed the attention of her mop, bucket and scrubbing brush.

Eventually I think mother decided that the Cane Hill recruitment resource had its drawbacks and she probably upped her hourly rate in order to secure cleaners from a less unconventional source.

Then she recruited Queenie, small and wiry with jet black eyes and as Irish as they come. Unlike any of the others, she did not appear to have a family name: 'Call me Queenie,' she demanded even of us children, so Queenie it was. I don't know how good she was at cleaning, but she was everything at communication that reserved Mrs Potter was not. Her hours were either longer or just later than her predecessor's: perhaps that was when she could fit us in. On her days, she was there when I got back from school and sometimes when my father got back from his work. One only had to go into the room in which she was working for Queenie's garrulous nature to take precedence over any cleaning or tidying.

Penthusiasm

Although she had no connection with any lunatic asylum, she too could be unnervingly unpredictable. I must have been about nine when, in the midst of telling me some complicated story about her family back in Ireland, she took from her pocket a shiny tin box, opened it and offered me a roll-up cigarette. Then she put another half-smoked one in her mouth, lit it for a few puffs and then stubbed it out on the shiny box. I'd have loved to have accepted her cigarette offer, but children's smoking was strictly to be performed behind the bicycle sheds at school and other similarly discreet places and not in front of adults! Both my parents smoked, as did almost everyone in those days, but not young children (or not officially). I never told anyone about Queenie's amazing 'illegal' offer: it was our secret, I suppose.

Apart from chatting, Queenie liked tidying more than cleaning. While it was no show-home, our house appeared to me to be tidy enough: my bedroom was the sole exception. But that didn't stop Queenie from moving almost everything just slightly on the shelves and mantelpiece. Duster in hand, she moved the wooden carved lady ornament to face the front, not slightly sideways, and the clock to be dead in the middle and not to one side. It annoyed my mother on the few occasions she noticed these miniscule changes. Not because she didn't like the readjustments (which were hardly noticeable) but because it meant that Queenie had spent less time on her hands and knees scrubbing the scullery floor.

Then there was the occasion when, on getting back from school, I discovered Queenie carefully lining up all the little die-cast cars in my bedroom's toy garage. These cars were among the most prized toys I owned and at least once a day were pushed round on the lino floor along an improvised circuit of chalked roads in races of several laps. But until then, they had never ever been arranged neatly in lines in their box-cum garage, according to size, colour or anything else. Love or not, they'd just been piled in together and the lid (garage-roof) closed on top of them.

My first reaction was to be taken aback by Queenie's intrusion into my private automobile fantasy. But her chatty, forthright approach was disarming and quite quickly we were discussing whether a Triumph TR2 was better than an MGA in the corners or why I preferred the Austin Healey to the Ferrari. She clearly knew nothing about cars in reality, but she managed to maintain a conversation by asking questions which got me thinking. 'Why is there a band of yellow on the front of that one?' (*A Vanwall*) 'Where do those red ones come from?' (*Maserati - Italy*).

No adult before - or since - engaged with me so effectively in my fantasy world of motorsport. I probably would have allowed her to choose cars for her own team - to race against my favourites - if we hadn't been interrupted by the sound of someone coming upstairs. Queenie was busy wiping windows with her duster by the time my mother was in the doorway, checking on what was taking her so long. 'These windows were really grimy. I've already been over them all once,' she chirruped with staggering ease.

I doubt that my mother was taken in but she was silenced by the deceit!

'I'm just going to finish the bathroom,' Queenie added promptly before her employer's jaw had finished dropping, and she was out of my room and across the hall. Mother looked at me and then at the garage of cars. Speechless, she turned and went back downstairs, leaving me to luxuriate in the new bond of deceit which Queenie had somehow forged between us.

Like Mrs Potter, Queenie was with us for some years, artfully avoiding confrontation with my mother who continued to be both somewhat dissatisfied and rather suspicious of the sweet-talker. That her blarney cut no ice with the mistress of the house was clear, but it gave her an edge that was hard to blunt.

When I was eleven I was sent to boarding school, and by the end of my first or second term, Queenie had been replaced by Mrs Balint, a recent refugee, who spoke with a very strong Eastern European accent and worked without pausing. I saw her very infrequently because I was only around during

Penthusiasm

school holidays and often Mrs Balint was having her own holidays at the same time.

In any case, not long afterwards, we moved from that house to a modern, new home that seemed to need less cleaning and certainly had no scullery floor. Down a remote rural cul-de-sac, it was not at all conveniently situated for home helps. My mother decided that she would manage without much outside assistance, bought a newer, better vacuum cleaner and the days of chars were really over.

Steve Hoselitz

SWEET REVENGE

Exterminating her husband had been on her mind for many years. After every beating, the urge became stronger and stronger. Getting away with it wasn't really a concern; it was the thought of revenge that consumed her mind, body and soul. Sometimes, her bruised, violated limbs wrestled with thoughts of his demise. But just how to do it?

One night, as she lay huddled on the cosy suburban bedroom floor, after yet another session of violence, the temptation to crawl to the kitchen and return with the meat knife was more overwhelming than ever. The one thing that stopped her was the thought that she may stab him and not actually kill him. Then she would never escape.

Hours of research on the internet gave her hope of undetectable substances that could be concealed in his food. A decision was finally made. She'd trawled the ironmongers shops, bought unnecessary gardening equipment and finally purchased an ideal product. One that would act fast, leave no trace, and end her years of abuse and suffering forever.

The mere fact that it was there, hidden in the garden shed, lifted her spirits, and the terror of last night's Southern Comfort beating seemed a little less painful. As always, he'd tried to make amends the next day, full of apologies and promises to change his ways. They fell on deaf ears. She'd heard it a thousand times. He helped with the washing up and took the children to school. He'd made her a coffee, which she drank with smugness, knowing that she'd found an answer.

The white china coffee mug, her favourite, gripped in her fingers, she inhaled the sweet aroma and swallowed. In seconds, her hand grasped her neck as she felt the vice-like grip constricting her throat. She couldn't breathe. Her heart raced out of control and her eyes bulged. Her gasps became unbearable. As she fell to the cold tiled kitchen floor, she caught a glimpse of his smirking face watching her through the kitchen window.

Margaret Payne

Penthusiasm

NO – REALLY!

You don't want to be thinking about microbes.
If you did you'd go right off your head,
'cos it seems they're around in their billions
- on your hands - up your nose – in your bed.

Of course, you can't see them – they're tiny,
Unless under a microbe-os-cope,
I mean - our forebears were blissfully ignorant,
and – let's face it – they all seemed to cope.

So, best not to think of it, really,
How they're swarming all over your loo,
Your taps and your eyebrows, your doorknobs,
Your dishcloths and - yes – over you!

No, really, please don't start to worry,
On the whole they will do you no harm,
And they're – probably - really - quite friendly,
So – keep calm – there's no need for alarm.

Put it out of your mind, I implore you.
Allow it no more of your time,
Think of Cif and of bleach and those spray things,
They'll all get to work on the grime.

Just don't put your hands on a banister,
Especially one in a store,
and don't think of the thousands of people
whose microby hands went before.

Crumbs – I seem to have started a panic.
It was just that I wanted to share,
Yes, I wear rubber gloves and a face mask,
But it's just that I like to take care.

Seven Monmouthshire Writers

'Pandemonium sets in around Chelsea.'
Today's headline on BBC News
Fumigation is rife, from John O'Groats up to Fife,
and YouTube is blowing a fuse!

Sainsbury's run out of Dettol,
and everyone's scrubbing at home.
Except some, taking hols out in Italy,
Perhaps the microbes are weaker in Rome?

I think I should keep a low profile,
But I've good news to fill you with hope,
because Donald has found the solution,
and he's washing his mouth out with soap!

Louise Longworth

Penthusiasm

EARLY SEPTEMBER MORNING IN NORMANDY 1984

As the mist cleared, I saw the eerie faint silhouette of our destination gradually unfold. The silence, the dampness, and the haze folded around us like a magical cloak. We drove nearer. The enormity of the site before us was breathtaking.

The early morning tide was away at play, leaving only the glistening sand and salt marshes surrounding the Mount. Nobody had ventured on the beach yet. The only movement were the munching sheep and the sea-gulls flying overhead squawking their greeting. Their French greeting. Our trip was nearly at an end as Mont Saint Michel towered along the shoreline before us.

The gently sloping medieval defence walls of the abbey drew my gaze unavoidably to the golden statue of the Archangel Michael on the tip of the monastery spire. Was he tempting us to venture within these ancient walls? Yes, who could resist such a magnificent place? We parked our motor-bike in the huge empty car-park, locked up our helmets, and took the long walk along the cobbled causeway to the main gated entrance. The *Grand Rue*.

Archangel Michael's lure.

The *Grand Rue*. An upward cobbled moss-filled lane, overhung with grubby medieval stone buildings. Tiny lace edged windows. Hanging plants and barking dogs. A gentle stroll past dim alleyways and gated yards. Beautifully painted shrines inset high into the walls. A few chickens and goats belonging to the 40 or so inhabitants of the mount. Trees growing desperately out of walls and cliff edges. Old rickety wooden seats where we could sit and gaze at the splendid view beneath us. Higher up, sweet-smelling homemade refreshments to encourage the visitors to climb the steep steps to the monastery. Wrong. So utterly wrong.

At the gated entrance, we passed the newly-built ladies and gents toilets. An archway took us onto the *Grand Rue*, a cobbled narrow lane leading eventually to the 900 steps and the monastery. The *Rue* was hung with a maze of signs. Signs of every colour and shape. Some illuminated. Some decked in flags. Shop after shop after shop. We blinked in amazement. How could our expectations be so completely wrong? We followed the winding *Rue*. There were hundreds of tacky souvenir shops, dozens of confectioners, gaudy tee-shirts suspended on hangers, exclusive galleries and unaffordable jewellery establishments. Tempting smells filled our nostrils: crêpes, fresh coffee and warm bread. Expensive *a la carte* restaurants tucked into every possible corner stealing the dramatic scenery beyond. Occasionally we glimpsed a view of the shore below, and the small cottages belonging to the locals. By the time that we reached the Ancient Church of St Pierre, at the half way point, we decided not to climb the 900 steps to the monastery. We turned and pushed our way back through the excited noisy tourists now puffing their way upwards, clutching bottles of pop, toffee bars and French tokens of their visit. Sadly our illusions shattered and our heads spinning, we hurriedly searched for our now-hidden motor-bike and departed. A mile or so along the roadway, we stopped and turned back to look at Mont Saint Michel now bathed in brilliant chill sunshine, backed by puffy white clouds. A memory to savour. Archangel Michael did not impress us with his temptation.

Margaret Payne

Penthusiasm

MUSIC TO MY EARS

Neither of my parents was very musical and I don't remember any kind of gramophone at home when I was very little except for a dusty clockwork wind-up job, complete with a small tin of needles which did more harm than good to the few 78rpm records that lay around in their scruffy paper sleeves.

On Saturday mornings, my sister and I would stay in the kitchen close to the large crackly mains radio so we could listen to *Children's Favourites,* on the Light Programme (now Radio 2) hosted by Uncle Mac. *Teddy Bear's Picnic* and other such delights were regular offerings.

The first record I bought was a 78: *Wonderful, Wonderful Copenhagen*, sung by Danny Kaye. I didn't buy another for quite a few years until 45s were around. By then I was mesmerised by *My Friend the Witchdoctor*: what impeccable taste I had.

My mother could sometimes be heard singing a snatch of something from *Salad Days – If I should happen to find you* - before her two horrid children ran in to the room wheeling and screeching, our hands clamped over our ears like two lunatics. Mother didn't have a really good voice, but it didn't warrant the severe criticism implied by our reaction!

Years later, mother and son would sit quietly side by side in the lounge listening to what was now a stereo system playing Flanders and Swann's *At the Drop of a Hat*. We listened to it so often I'm still almost word perfect. *The big six-wheeler, scarlet painted, London Transport, diesel engined, ninety-seven horsepower omnibus...* For me it was the start of an enduring love of comic songs. Want a faithful rendition of Tom Lehrer's *Vatican Rag*? OK. I'll save that for later...

If anything, my father appeared even less musical than Mum. The exception was Christmas Day when out of a large box in the attic would come a complicated piano accordion with lovely but fake mother-of-pearl detailing which he would shyly play, using both the keyboard - with his right hand - and an amazing array of unmarked chord buttons with his left, all the while closing and opening the enormous fan-like bellows in a fluid, practised motion. It was a highly impressive display of a hidden talent which, for some reason I never fathomed, he kept jealously hidden on every other day of the year.

My sister was in the school recorder group. And for a brief period I was keen on the trumpet, for which I showed some aptitude. What I really wanted to play was not on offer at my school: the guitar. Later I bought a second-hand flamenco guitar and the Chet Atkins' *A Tune A Day Tutor* book... *Freight train, freight train...*

I'm sure I would have been an internationally famous pop star with girlfriends galore if I hadn't been left-handed and almost tone deaf.

Steve Hoselitz

Penthusiasm

A FISHY TALE

Goldfish, Silverfish, Whitebait, Grayling
Red Snapper, Black fin, Blue-ray - Carp.

Catfish, Dogfish, Sea robin, Horse-fish
Cow-fish, Lion-fish, Parrot-fish - Koi.

Bluntnose, Thorntail, Lungfish, Fingerfish,
Bristlemouth, Bullhead, Fathead Skate.

Candle-fish, Electric Ray, Velvet-belly Lantern Shark,
Flashlight-fish, Sun-fish, Lamphrey - all aglow.

Guitar- fish, Rock-fish, Drum-fish, Banjo-fish,
Clown-fish, Gibber-fish, Cobbler - then there's Gar.

Swordfish, Stingray, and the Dagger-Toothed Conger
Snapper-fish, Knife-fish, Cut-throat Eel.

Angel-fish, Ghost-fish, Cherub-fish, Spook-fish
Sun-fish, Moon-fish, Goblin-fish -Ghoul.

Ale-wife, Bar- fish, Glass-fish, Ice-fish,
Large-mouth Bass fish - often followed by a Grunt

Tommy-ruff, Turbot, and then there's Tern and Tuna,
Haddock, - Oh! and Herring - Halibut and Hake.

>No?
>So,

If there's nothing in my repertoire you fancy for your lunch-box –
Please reconsider. If I beg you – will you stay?
See, when I'd been and sold my sole, I knew I was a Dab hand,
'Cos there's another load of Pollocks on the way!

Louise Longworth

Seven Monmouthshire Writers

THE STORM

This morning. A cold chill morning. Jim tumbled out of his bed, dressed, put on his new trainers and silently left the house by the back door. He left a neatly folded note to his family, leaning against a vase of lilac. Lilac was his mum's favourite flower. She loved the smell, and when he was young, he'd help her reach the branches of the neighbour's tree. They would laugh and tease each other about 'stealing' the neighbour's flowers, as his mum arranged them in large ornate vases around the house. That was so long ago, when he could think straight. When his mind wasn't scrambled and tormented by even the easiest daily chores. Before his head filled with voices, confusing his actions and decisions. He was of use to nobody. He was a drain on his parents. He had failed as a son. Now he had accepted his fate, knowing it was the right thing to do. No going back now, Jim, he told himself.

He reached the bridge. The bridge he has crossed a thousand times, on foot, on his old rickety scooter and more recently on his push bike. The bridge was beckoning him. The roads were silent, only the call of an overhead seagull screeched high above. He climbed the wall easily, slowly edging his way to the centre of the bridge. The highest point. Below him the grey swirling water lapped against the rocks. Jim was not afraid. He glanced at the church clock opposite. It would strike six soon. On the sixth stroke, he would open his arms and fly. Fly to a better tomorrow. Fly to freedom. He hoped his parents would forgive him. He could smell the sweet scent of lilac as the sixth toll echoed around him. And he was gone...

Margaret Payne

Penthusiasm

A RECIPE FOR SUCCESS

The last time I had much to do with poetry, the lines scanned, the words rhymed and the whole thing had a rhythm you could beat out on the knees of your school uniform trousers so you could reach the end at the same time as everyone else – but poetry has changed and like so many other things today, anything goes; rhyme and rhythm or no rhyme and rhythm, lines of different lengths – grammar, capitals and punctuation open, optional or totally omitted.

With an Eisteddfod approaching, the group's task is to write shape poems – no need for rhyme, rhythm or meaning but - the words must make a shape on the page. H wrote a haunting, lyrical poem of love portrayed as a lock of hair and written in a circle. Mortification - why was I the only one to endeavour to read it in a circle? I saw the words and instant dyslexia set in. Not only was I deaf from a fiendish ear infection – every day sounds muffled by internal malfunctioning, but now my eyes were joining in. They refused to communicate anything other than a random jumble of words and phrases, until I am tipped the wink to 'read across' and instantly all returns to normal; still deaf but eyes and brain once more in synch. So I rack my brains and chew my metaphorical pencil, hoping for inspiration, whilst I listen to the swish and crackle inside my head as the antibiotics fight a valiant fight to return me to the normal hearing world.

What shape the poem? It's St David's Day, so how about a daffodil? The shape is beyond me and the words have already been done unbeatably by William Wordsworth – so not a complete philistine. Pragmatism sets in.

How about a bedside lamp or a tube of toothpaste; a slipper, a glass of water or a packet of biscuits? Inspiration strikes:

Seven Monmouthshire Writers

Beat   butter,   sugar,   flour and   egg
Use a silicone spatula to scrape out the dregs,
Then place in the oven - in a well- lined tin.
You'll know when it's done by a skewer poked in.
Add jam, cream and icing - before neatly slicing.
Then put it on a plate in the middle of the table and let
everybody help themselves.

Anna Hitch

Penthusiasm

THE WEDDING

We'd spent just over a year together, and so I had no hesitation in agreeing to marry him. The proposal was so romantic. We were in a beautiful little boat, under a star-laden sky and he told me that I was beautiful and began to serenade me. I returned the compliment, telling him how much I adored his elegant sweet song.

Buying a ring was our first worry. Money wasn't a problem at all, we had plenty. But whilst walking in a bong tree wood, we met a little pig, who gladly sold us his nose ring for a very reasonable shilling.

The very next day we climbed the hill and found a turkey who married us. We were so happy dancing on the sand in the moon light, after enjoying a wedding feast of mince and quince, easily eaten with a runcible spoon. We never did finish the jar of honey.

Margaret Payne

Seven Monmouthshire Writers

ARTHUR'S MARTHA

(after Henry Wadsworth Longfellow)

By the store of Tesco Local
Clutching flowers her daughter bought her
At the entrance to a pound shop
In the foul persistent rainstorm
Arthur's Martha stood and waited.
Waited as the clock ticked faster.

All the street dark, dank and windswept
All the ground awash with litter.
Precinct packed with hell-bent shoppers
Past the plate-glass-glitz emporia
Past the perfect mannequin temptings.
Past the cafés peddling pizza.

Eastward roars the mighty high road
Song of birds eclipsed and distant
Boots hit haste-reflecting puddles
Headless torsos wearing brollies
Heedless in the rush for bargains
Arthur's Martha stands there - waiting.

Now - a sudden burst of sunshine
Cautious checking – hands out-stretching
Expressions softening, paces slackening
Droplets fly as brollies folding.
Martha scans oncoming figures,
None the right one. Still she's waiting.

Sudden bear hug - 'I'm so sorry
Clutch went. AA saved the day,'
Arthur's Martha stands there, radiant,
Heart so full - yes it's today!
Eyes a little damp - but twinkling
Hands clasped - warm - they haste away.

Penthusiasm

At last their plans come to fruition,
At last the lovers see their way,
At last their dreams will find fulfilment,
their treasured secret tucked away.
For Martha's Arthur and Arthur's Martha,
Today's the day that they'll make pay.

The day they've longed for, prayed for, hoped for.
The day they rob the bank.
Whey Hey!

Louise Longworth

THE SMILE

It's Mother's Day in three days' time. Trying to avoid it is very difficult with reminders in just about every window. I recently lost my Mum. It's difficult. I miss her. Lost, but she is still with me. She loved me, I know that. And I loved her. Not only on Mother's Day.

It's Mother's Day in two days time. Last Monday I made the decision to clear Mum's wardrobe. It had to be done. Things she loved to wear. Things bought on day trips and shopping sprees. I carefully folded the things for the charity shop. Without hesitating or peeping back into the bags, I delivered them straightaway.

It's Mother's Day today. I had to go to the post office. I pass the new display in the Red Cross Charity Shop. There in the window, the model stood proudly in her new spring outfit. A yellow tee shirt slung with an orange jacket and a brown patchwork design M&S skirt. My Mum's skirt. I was transfixed. I couldn't move. I felt a lurch in the stomach with both surprise and sadness. Mum would be amused to see that model posing back at me. I think she was sending me a smile for Mother's Day. Thank you, Mum. You always did like that skirt.

Margaret Payne

Penthusiasm

WHEN I WAS YOUNGER

When I was younger, I used to believe that through tolerance, sharing and equality of opportunity, we could make the world a better place. Deep down I perhaps still believe that, but I'm not sure how we're going to get there now.

So what has changed? Well, I guess the single most destructive force in my lifetime has been the creed of Margaret Thatcher and all those who glory in her wake. Her messages, that there's no such thing as society and that greed is good, are the direct opposite of everything I still believe.

Here's some context. My parents were Jewish refugees from Hitler's Europe. They met in Britain, having narrowly escaped extermination. They believed until their dying days that Britain was a land of fairness and tolerance, in sharp contrast to the discrimination they had encountered in mainland Europe.

What I see now is starting to smell a *little* like what I think my parents experienced in their youth. So many of the 'fair and tolerant' British people are now comfortable with hateful messages like 'grasping immigrants jumping queues and choking the NHS'. So many people will tell you in total sincerity of someone to whom it has happened. Warped hearsay has become fact; a modern myth feeding on the concept of 'them and us'. Scarily, these messages are not that dissimilar to those on which Hitler's hateful creed fed. Grasping immigrants, grasping Jews? Is it so different?

This is far more widespread than UKIP's torrent of discriminatory hate: ordinary 'decent' people now openly talk about floods of immigrants, convinced by negative media coverage rather than their own experiences. Isn't it strange that here in uncrowded, overwhelmingly white Wales, UKIP has still managed to become the second largest party. And we are about to leave the EU for similar negative, xenophobic reasons. Perhaps this is because we are an island nation; perhaps because deep down we are lamenting our loss of empire and world status; perhaps because, unlike any other

European nation, we have not experienced occupation by a foreign power for almost 1,000 years.

Whatever the reason, I'm finding it harder and harder to be proud of the nation that afforded my parents sanctuary, without which I would not have existed.

Born in the late 1940s, I grew up with the songs of the sixties: peace, love, happiness. Themes which were, yes, naïve, unrealistic, idealistic, carefree. They were gentle and aspirational, which is perhaps why they were so fragile.

By contrast what do today's young, our future, have as their overarching themes? Debt? Unemployment or unskilled work? The struggle for housing? Gadgetry? It seems all so miserable and so mercenary. So how, I really wonder, are we ever going to build a society where we share and care rather than hate and berate?

We, the British, have more than enough of everything, absolutely everything. But we seem to have lost the ability to share it fairly among ourselves and we certainly are losing the ability to show compassion in the place of greed.

In the argot of the moment, it's at least 1 – 0 to the Thatcherites and I fear our 90 minutes are nearly up. Was it all a fairy story: that which I believed so passionately? Or was it, is it, a fair story?

Steve Hoselitz

Penthusiasm

THE SPONGE BAG

Today I said goodbye to an old friend. Ten years and two months is a good life span for an ordinary sponge bag. The flowers on its cover have faded over the years – no longer the vivid hues of its youth. Its cover is still intact but yellowed foam is seeping through cracks in the plastic lining, as serum seeps from newly-sutured wounds.

It has travelled with me to France, to Italy, to Canada and the Canaries. On arrival at Bucharest airport, its contents were inspected by a Romanian soldier armed with a machine gun. It was small enough to fit neatly into any luggage but large enough to take everything I might need for two weeks away. Even at home my make-up has rested within its zippered confines – just in case.

I bought it, for shame's sake, in July 1999 along with new dressing gown and slippers. Nobody goes into hospital for cold surgery with worn slippers, a threadbare dressing gown and a sponge bag made out of a polythene bag. I filled it with soap and flannel for a stranger to wipe away the splashes of iodine, make-up to conceal the pale face of fear and perfume to mask the scent of sickness.

The sponge bag is beyond repair, but I am here. Cut and repaired, scarred inside and out, bearing witness that although a diagnosis can be devastating, some of us live to fight on, protesting confidence in our future...but always keeping a decent sponge bag, packed and ready – just in case.

Anna Hitch

'WHY DIDN'T YOU CALL ME?'

'Why didn't you call me?' Paula had waited so long to ask Ricky that question. And now there she was between aisles 6 and 7 in the superstore where 'good food costs less, pat pat', face to face with a blast from the past, who was clutching a very large bottle of cheap ketchup.

She stared at his never-forgotten blue eyes, mesmerised by the intensity of their colour and gaze. She held her breath. Would her curiosity finally be quenched after so many years? Just a simple question.

Ricky glared. Not a single flicker of recognition registered. Not an inkling. Who the hell was she? Most of his Ricky the Rocker days were spent in a haze between Manchester and Macclesfield in the arms of faceless, nameless, sex-mad, groupies. Damn. Come on, Ricky boy, dig into the soul and come up with something profound. Beads of sweat oozed from his top lip. His very fat top lip, which now matched the rest of his flabby body, along with the balding head and ruddy drunken complexion. He grasped the ketchup bottle firmly and lied, 'Oh babe, yeah, we did have some fun, eh? Many a day I cursed that bloody landlady for chucking me Levi's in the old washing machine before checking me pockets. Wretched woman! All I was left with was a ball of sodden paper. Shame, real shame.'

Wow, that was a goodun, he mused, mentally patting himself on the sweat-trickled back. A memory flash shot through him. Girls screaming and clambering, offering mind-blowing propositions and nights of passion. A night with Ricky the Rocker. Those were the days. Now long gone.

Paula sighed pessimistically, Ricky shook his head in confusion, and a rather buxom black-rooted blonde, wearing a tee-shirt announcing that she was 'a retired groupie', shouted from the check out.

'Dick, Dick, come on! We ain't got all bloody day. You got the ketchup?'

Ricky, now alias Dick, turned as scarlet as his purchase. He

Penthusiasm

had to make his escape. The retired groupie wasn't the most patient of women.

'Sorry, eeerrmm, sorry babe, gotta go, summoned by the boss. Nice seeing ya. Take care. Good old days, eh?'

'Good old days, yeah, great times,' replied Paula. 'I've gotta go too, my lift is here.'

Ricky the Rocker made a hasty, relieved retreat.

'Blimey, Mum, who was that old geezer I saw you talking to?'

'Him? Oh, nobody important. A guitarist I knew once. One crazy night and he never called me,' Paula said gazing lovingly at her son.

'His loss,' joked the lad with the stunning deep blue eyes.

'Yeah, come on, Ricky, drive me home.'

Margaret Payne

Seven Monmouthshire Writers

ORDINARY PEOPLE

Written with one of Penelope Keith's 'supercilious character' voices in mind

You know, the nobodies they mention on the telly,
I'd nothing else to do so thought I'd look,
but where to start? I know they're out there in their millions,
plenty of material for a book.

So of course I turned to Google, as we all do,
for a definition that would help me in my search
'Unexceptional'. Like the people I see standing in that bus queue?
Of course - oh, this is easy - this research.

So I made a start on that and went to Asda,
bought some bits and bobs and joined the line,
Oh yes - here comes a very dear old lady,
typically ordinary, she'll do fine.

I waited 'til she'd bought her tins of cat food,
then I said about me trying to write a book,
asked her what it felt like - being ordinary,
would she help me to research - 'and take a look?'

We went and had a coffee and a doughnut,
(that's what ordinary people, I think - eat,)
then she started to embark upon her life's tale
 - and had me spellbound - as I sat there in my seat

She'd only driven through the Blitz in wartime London.
An ambulance that is, through bombs and flak,
had her home blown up, and lost all her possessions,
joined the WAAF - and met her airman - name of Jack.

Penthusiasm

OK - well – Jack, at least, you'd label 'ordinary',
'cos in Civvy Street - he swept them - clean and bright . .
mmm . . .'cept they gave him an award for volunteering
in a shelter for the homeless every night.

So I thanked the lady humbly for her input,
I shall keep in touch and put her in the book.
An example of not judging a book's cover.
Then I said goodbye, and carried on to look.

Where next? . . Oh – yes ! I'll find some in a - Chip Shop,
good place to find an ordinary chap,
so I consulted Yellow Pages and I found one
thought I'd play the part, put on an old flat cap.

Drove jalopy to the area suggested,
didn't need to ask directions – followed nose!
Oh yes, - spoilt for choice I'll be here – see the chaps there,
good job I'd practised 'ordinary' – how to pose.

Got chatting to a fellow in a 'track suit',
great candidate for 'ordinary' - certain fact,
. . . 'til he told me about his coaching - wheelchair football
after work. And he's a brickie – must be whacked!

As I got back in the Roller with my supper
I thought, this ain't so easy, Tara – think again.
You must have been unlucky with your choices,
they're out there in their thousands – 'ordinary' men.

I've now been looking for a year – but I'm disheartened.
Where are the ordinary nobodies I seek?
Everyone I question is extra-ordinary
. . . and the outlook for my book is pretty bleak.

Mothers, youngsters, granddads, fathers, grandmas,
described as 'ordinary' by the pundits on the box,

Seven Monmouthshire Writers

Invisible - but doing things remarkable
and helping other people through life's knocks.

Their stories rarely make it to the front page.
Doing unsolicited helpful things unsung
Fostering and caring, giving blood, donating organs
 - and giving precious time to old and young

Raising money for a thousand different causes,
by a thousand different efforts, big and small
but when asked if they were special, they'd just chuckle,
and say – 'Nah! Never' - but they're there for one and all.

I'm still going to write the book, so keep a look out,
but the title's changed, as you may well have guessed,
because I've yet to meet an 'ordinary' person, and -
I'm petitioning to get the stupid word suppressed.

Louise Longworth

ABOUT THE PUBLISHERS

Saron Publishers has been in existence for about ten years, producing niche magazines. Our first venture into books took place last year when we published *The Meanderings of Bing* by Tim Harnden-Taylor. Further publications planned for 2017 include *The Ramblings of Bing*, the second volume in the *Lines From My Forehead* series, and *Frank*, a novel by Julie Hamill, author of *Fifteen Minutes With You*.

Join our mailing list by emailing info@saronpublishers.co.uk. We promise no spam ever.

Visit our website saronpublishers.co.uk to keep up to date and to read reviews of what we've been reading and enjoying. You can also enjoy the occasional offer of a free Bing chapter.

Follow us on Facebook @saronpublishers.
Follow us on Twitter @SaronPublishers.